The Girl in the White Dress

by

Paul Barrell

First Published February 2020

Printed by Amazon.

Cover design and graphics advice Craig Armstrong.

Typesetting and proofreading Chris Parker.

In memory of Terry B.

Thanks for the stories.

'Landfall and departure mark the rhythmical swing of a seaman's life and of a ship's career. From land to land is the most concise definition of a ship's earthly fate.'

Joseph Conrad 'The Mirror of the Sea.'

'Sometimes in life things happen to us that are beyond our control. Sometimes they defy explanation.

You don't need to believe in ghosts or the supernatural, just believe in the universe and the threads of random chance that link us all together.'

Paul Barrell 2019

I sank so far down into a black well of dreams that I had to claw my way to the surface to wake up…

1974

I slipped silently off my bunk and opened the cabin door. My pulse quickened, a second passed, then another. I took a deep breath and peered down the dimly lit corridor.

I had to go.

Now.

My bare feet sank into the thick blue and gold carpet and whenever the ship rolled, I gripped the polished handrails for support. I hurried passed the porters' lift where the stench of fried meat mingled with something putrid and fecal. The combination of the two smells made me gag. I swallowed hard, pushing down the bile that rose in my throat.

I ran like my life depended on it, until I reached the bottom of a wide staircase.

At the top, I stood for a moment under a huge mural of a crowned Queen, before I turned left down another endless passageway. On a higher deck I ran into a trolley laden with ice buckets and wine glasses, and swerved past the outstretched arm of an irate porter, who fired abuse at me as I passed.

Adult voices followed me everywhere and I prayed my parents were still upstairs enjoying the Captain's party. Over the last three weeks, my father had proved himself to be a formidable drinking companion, ingratiating himself with a rowdy crowd from Essex. The pinnacle of his achievements was his winning performance in the limbo competition, where, with his blonde curly hair, yellow hula-hula skirt and bow legs, he looked like a native of some far-off desert island. For me it was just more ritual embarrassment.

I continued along a rubber-matted external walkway, then through a heavy safety door. Back in the cosseted warmth of the ship, I scurried between tables and chairs until I reached the forward lounges. In the distance, the ship's bow rose and fell, her flag snapping in the gusting wind as sea spray crashed against the plexiglass. I stopped to catch my breath. I could go no further; the red lettering over the next door read: "No Admittance - Crew Only".

I caught my reflection, a ghostly face framed by a mop of hair peering through the window as a starburst of rockets lit up the night sky. Now the bridge and crib tables were deserted, incongruous shapes lit occasionally by orange and green neon lighting that pulsed intermittently along grey bulkhead walls. I crouched down behind the stage, opened a small hatch and crawled into the storage compartment.

The ship's engines hummed and throbbed under my hands and the odour of diesel and bilge caught in my throat. It took a while for my eyes to adjust to the gloom.

'Where are you?' I whispered.

Silence.

I spoke again, a little louder this time.

Still no answer.

I fought back tears and was about to leave, when…

'Over here.'

Her voice was warm like soothing honey.

I scrambled over lifejackets and sunbed cushions to the far corner: our place. She grabbed my hand and the small pen torch I held illuminated her face. She was a mixture of contradictions, precocious, untamed and I was mesmerised by her ice blue eyes, identical to the colour of the party garland that hung loosely from her shoulders.

I caressed her cheek and an electric charge travelled from my fingertips to somewhere deep inside. Intense heat emanated from every pore of her body and I wondered if she was sick; of course she wasn't, I was just too young to recognise the tell-tale signs of desire. She grabbed my arm tightly.

'Have you got it?'

I reached into my pocket and withdrew a small object.

She sat cross-legged and leaned against my shoulder.

'I knew you could do it.'

I preened like a peacock, placed the package in her palm and felt her warm breath on my face as she ran her fingers over the object.

'Shine the torch over here so I can see it properly.'

My hand trembled as I tried to hold the torch steady.

'It's beautiful!' she gasped.

I shrugged my shoulders.

She tugged my arm.

'Can I keep it?'

'You said it was only…'

Her voice was a little firmer this time.

'Can I keep it?'

I hesitated. This wasn't the plan we had discussed. Then I relented because I didn't want her to get angry again.

'You must never tell anyone I gave it to you. Promise me. Cross your heart and hope to die.'

She placed her arms theatrically across her chest.

'I promise I will never tell anyone, as long as I live.'

I leaned closer and in the dark our lips touched as we mimicked the famous film stars, we watched together night after night in the ship's cinema. She tried to break away but I clung to her, felt her heart beat and breathed in her scent. Our holiday would soon be at an end, we would return to our families, our towns, our separate lives. They were insurmountable hurdles and I feared, after tonight, I might never see her again.

I was awakened by a sharp prod in my ribs. She brushed her lips against my ear.

'Wake up, we have to go. It'll be morning soon.'

I was drowsy. How long had I been asleep? When I was fully awake, I realised I was desperately thirsty. I swallowed hard.

'I need a drink.'

She nodded and took my hand.

'Come on, follow me' and we left the crawlspace for the last time.

There were two narrow flights of steep stairs to be negotiated so I knew I was heading towards the upper decks. But where? My sight was restricted by a bandana she had tied round my head and she laughed as if mocking me. I stumbled and before I could regain my composure a door blew open and a salty sea spray whipped my face. She liked games, especially when she was in control and she tugged my hand to hurry me along.

'Over here. Your special prize awaits,' then, in a whisper, 'I promised, didn't I?'

When she spoke like this I surrendered completely, but there was something in her tone this evening that troubled me. Her moods swung like a pendulum, and now she seemed cruel and reckless. I had done exactly as she requested, but I sensed this might not be a game at all. She leaned in close and I smelt her breath, sweet like toffee, and in an instant felt her hands grip my shoulders. She spun me round, once, twice, three times until I felt dizzy. I wanted to tell her to stop, but the words would not come. Instead I remembered a game we played in the quad at school, when we ran round the broken broom handle ten times, before trying to stand on it. That was how I felt now, giddy and disorientated.

'Please, stop!' I shouted into the dark night.

She caught me and her lips brushed my neck. I froze.

'No, not yet. Just a little further,' and she placed my hand on her pert breast.

'Do you like that, French boy?'

I left my hand there a little too long and she brushed it aside. This was another of her games, she liked to tease. I tried to convince myself there was nothing serious amiss, but deep inside I knew tonight she wasn't to be trusted.

We stepped outside into a biting wind that made me shiver. The lifeboats jangled overhead and I smelled the acrid diesel as it belched from the tall funnels. I shuffled after her like a shackled slave until I no longer felt the grainy wood of the deck under my feet. It took a moment for me to recognise the smooth texture of tiles.

The pool.

She removed the bandana with a magician's flourish, a foghorn sounded and in the seconds that followed as my eyes struggled to focus I sensed her move behind me. In a matter of moments, I felt her hand in the small of my back and in what seemed like slow motion I tumbled forward, my arms outstretched. It was OK I thought, I can swim, and I braced myself, waited for my legs to hit the icy water.

The girl looked down at me for a few seconds and then...

...I woke up drenched in sweat.

1

2005

The flashlight faltered and the corner of the loft plunged into darkness once more. I shifted my position on the narrow wooden beam and my muscles twitched as I held a pose an Olympic gymnast would have been proud of as I cursed under my breath.

'Shit, shit, shit!'

I had been looking forward to a celebratory drink in a local pub and my favourite takeaway; instead, I was halfway through unpacking every object I owned, the flotsam and jetsam of my life. Our lives.

Armistice Day. My birthday.

I smacked my open hand against the base of the torch, the beam of light returned and once more I shone it into the dark recesses of the chest.

Careful.

It was a delicate operation and I tugged carefully at the card. In the stillness I heard my mother's voice, her words of counsel. Her parent's house backed onto a graveyard and whenever I pushed the boundaries in my expanding world and dug too deep under the ancient wall for a shard of old animal bone or a Victorian bottle, my mother would stand at the French doors and recite an old English proverb.

'But, curiosity ONLY killed the cat!' I would shout back and we would both laugh.

We laughed a lot then, especially when grandad loosened his braces and pretended to hurdle the washing line, a feat I never saw him achieve because the miracle only occurred after Sunday lunch when my back was turned.

A high-pitched scream shattered my childhood memories and I scurried backwards, scraping elbows and knees along dusty beams; the candy floss insulation with its armoury of glass-like shards, a deadly swamp below.

'Dad! Dad! Where are you?'

The hairs on my neck bristled as I lowered myself down, but my weight was slightly off-centre and the loft ladder wobbled for a second as my trembling hands fought to stabilise it.

Another scream.

'I'm coming!' I shouted as my feet groped for the floor below.

I ducked under the ladder, ran along the landing past the small room that housed an antiquated WC, a room that already spooked my daughter, and skidded into her bedroom. The glow of her bedside light illuminated the far wall, already covered with a collage of galloping ponies and show jumpers. Hope sat in the middle of the bed, arms wrapped defensively around her knees, and wiped her nose with the back of her hand.

She looked up at me, tears streaming down her face.

'I can't sleep. The wind sounds like a hundred monsters clawing at my window.'

The removal van with our possessions arrived yesterday, a day late. There were no apologies from the two Neanderthal removal men as they deposited most of our belongings on the front drive before hurrying off to another job.

Hope chose the bedroom that overlooked the front garden and immediately she seemed drawn to the tree beneath her window.

'Can I climb it?'

I stood next to her and looked at its spindly branches, gnarled fingers reaching up towards the sky.

'It's not for climbing. The agent said it's a damson tree, they're quite rare and only bear fruit every other year.'

'What are damsons?'

'They're like small plums and can be made into jams or chutney.'

'Can we make jam?'

'Maybe next year. Look at the tree, I think we've missed the crop this year.'

A million questions and each one deserved a detailed answer. How I was going to cope?

I sat on the edge of her bed and she clung to me, like I was a solitary rock in a never-ending expanse of ocean. I caressed her cheek and studied her face. Her teeth chattered, and behind the fear, her hazel eyes were deep pools of innocence.

'Ssshhh. Come on, it's late, you must be exhausted after all the unpacking.'

Only a few cardboard boxes remained behind the door and I tried to praise her like her mother used to.

'You've done a great job, your room looks like you've lived here for years.'

Dust from the loft caught in my throat and I coughed.

'I'll leave the light on if you promise to go to sleep.'

Her features softened and she snuggled back down under her pink duvet. I stroked her hair tenderly.

'Dad.'

I knew what was coming.

'Yes.'

'I miss mummy.'

We all do.

'I know' I replied and moved on quickly before more complex questions started.

'Come on, let's say a prayer.'

I knelt by the side of her bed, closed my eyes and recited the Lord's prayer. I reflected that the regular trips to lay flowers on Anna's grave were not going to be possible now that we lived so far away.

'Amen.'

Hope peered at me over the top of her fingers.

'I'm going to miss my friends, and Bonny.'

A large lump formed in my throat.

'You'll make new ones. I promise. You know Bonny is really happy in her new home and the lady said she would write to us and let us know what mischief she's up to. Now go to sleep, there's school tomorrow and more unpacking when you get home.'

I leaned over the bed and planted a kiss on her sweaty brow.

'Sleep tight, I love you.'

Hope sprung up like a jack-in-a-box and there was a hint of impatience in my voice as I returned to her bedside.

'What?'

She reached up and threw her arms round my neck.

'Happy Birthday. I'm sorry I didn't bake you a cake. When mum was here, she always baked you a carrot cake with white icing.'

It was my favourite and I bit my bottom lip, my emotional rollercoaster in full swing.

'Yes she did, didn't she.'

She snuggled back under her duvet and elicited one last kiss on the tip of her nose before I turned towards the door. As I stepped out onto the landing and leant against the cool plaster my heart clenched; it was almost a physical sensation, a sharp stab of regret combined with fathomless sorrow. It was always the children that suffered most when families were ripped apart and I felt responsible for taking her away from her soulmate and best friend; they were inseparable.

I fought back tears and hurried downstairs to the kitchen. A heavy percussion of rain drummed against the window and I jumped as debris collided with the glass. The rear of the property overlooked a fast-running brook and the exterior security light illuminated four bedraggled sheep sheltering under a large oak tree. The agent had warned me that the weather in this area could be extremely volatile in the winter months.

The Peak District.

I paid sufficient interest in my history lessons at school to understand why textile manufacturers had established the silk industry in this region. It was a decision based on a microclimate that was perfectly suited to the lifecycle of silkworms. They thrived in damp weather and here the surrounding hills were littered with relics from the industrial revolution. In every direction the sky was pierced by the towers of derelict mills.

I rummaged haphazardly in a kitchen drawer until I found a suitable implement. I held the screwdriver up to the light like a wand and glanced again at the rain-whipped night through the window. The silk industry died many years ago, but the rain stayed.

I tiptoed back upstairs, past black and white prints of local geographical features, stopping halfway up to study a faded photograph of a man in a flat cap standing in front of a farmhouse. He was dwarfed by a huge snow drift and his diminutive stature gave the photograph an Arctic scale. The year inscribed in the left-hand corner was 1961. I remembered my parents said it was a harsh relentless winter.

You were born in the eye of a storm.

That year it started snowing on Christmas Eve and the sub-zero temperatures stayed until Easter. I subconsciously wrapped my arms round my chest. Was this what we should expect over the coming months?

I reached Hope's bedroom door, eased it open and peered in. She was curled up in a tight ball. I stood in the doorway and listened to her breathe, a sharp inhalation followed by a distinctive soft whistle, while outside branches tapped an eerie unwelcome staccato on the window pane. It was after midnight, the storm was gathering strength and I hoped she slept through until morning.

Rainwater surged down the guttering outside as I pulled myself up into the loft space again. The chest with my initials etched in gold on the lid sat alongside various suitcases and a pair of old skis. I picked up the flashlight and shone it once more into the empty space, letting the light play over the white card wedged in the corner. In the gloom I heard my mother again.

Curiosity killed the cat.

I shook my head ruefully, but undeterred reached down and slid the screwdriver underneath it.

It was about the size of a football programme and I brushed years of dust away with my cuff. The torch flickered casting creepy shadows in the eaves and I shuffled back towards the hatch where a light bulb hung from a roof joist.

The glow of light was weak but at least I could see the faded picture. The shipping line insignia was clearly visible, however the picture of the ship looked dated compared to the **new Superliners, floating behemoths that were** double or treble its size.

For a few seconds my mind searched for some distant reference point. There were a few words on the inside cover, but in the murky light they were hardly readable. A corner of the card had been torn or chewed and my skin crawled at the thought that it might be a rodent. I followed the thin beam of light as it scanned down a dinner menu. At the bottom of the page was part of a name, H. Cornw…Cornwall maybe? The head chef? I started reading through the menu: Filet of Plaice, Beurre Noisette, Pancake Diane with Chicken and Tongue, Chateaubriand with Béarnaise Sauce, and Pear Helene, just one of a multitude of exotic desserts. I ran my tongue over parched lips. We had only eaten a frugal tea this evening and the mouth-watering dishes triggered an unexpected flashback, a fleeting recollection, and in that moment, something rose to the surface, but as quickly as it had appeared it was gone.

2

1974

Oriana. Our holiday of a lifetime.

I was small for my age, my body still that of a boy rather than gawky adolescent and because I had my mother's wavy cappuccino hair and olive skin, I was frequently mistaken for a girl.

"Are you French?" complete strangers would ask my mother, when we were seen out together, which pleased her no end because she preferred the Gallic lifestyle and imagined that one day she would live in a rural French village with a fountain, a boulangerie and a café with alfresco dining.

My father worked in Fleet Street, an editor on a news desk, although I used to spin stories to the other kids in my class that he was a hot-shot reporter assigned to the most sadistic of crimes. I was quite an accomplished liar back then, not harmful stuff, just enough to make me seem interesting and gain me respect amongst my peers.

My parents probably loved each other once, although as I grew up it became apparent they inhabited completely different worlds. They argued constantly about money and dad's drinking, and in my teenage years I began to realise how little they had in common.

My mother was an alluring woman and had begun to forge a career in fashion and modelling. She was once described in a 1960s fashion magazine as a cross between a young Sophia Loren and Audrey Hepburn. I thought she had the best job in the world

and I never quite understood why she was with my
happy-go-lucky father. The cruise was to be her finest
hour, the whole ship her stage, where she could
portray her life as she would dearly liked to have
lived it. A new modelling assignment was currently
being discussed and as luck would have it a renowned
photographer was also travelling on the ship.
Someone who might be able to add a touch of
tropical glamour to her blossoming portfolio.

Parents should never have favourites, but I always
felt I was my mother's. My father was absent for
much of my childhood and it was thanks to her
persistence that I received a bursary and attended a
local private school. The Castle, as it was known, had
turrets and the prefects wore intimidating black
gowns. In my adolescent dreams they were like huge
vampire bats that swooped down from the
battlements to prey on the small and vulnerable. In
reality, they were the school's law enforcers and
dished out detentions to pupils who broke the rules.
There were a lot of rules at my school and from an
early age I wasn't good with them.

I was an inquisitive child, determined, with a vivid
imagination, all the traits of a true Scorpio. After
passing the eleven plus, I was moved from the junior
school into a class where all the boys were a year
older. I found the transition difficult, puberty loomed
and when the lights went out for an educational film
in the testosterone-filled geography room, discussions
turned to which girls they had felt up or supposedly
done it with. I listened intently, fascinated by their
sex talk and I longed to put what I heard into practice.

And now we were going on a cruise! The news
filled the whole family with excitement; three whole

weeks away. To an impressionable teenager, the Caribbean and its tropical archipelagos were the destination of dreams. A magical place with palm-fringed, Robinson Crusoe beaches, hillsides covered in sugar plantations, crystal blue lagoons and majestic colonial houses.

I remember our departure well. Families lined the decks, children shouted, a brass band thumped out a patriotic tune as the cruise ship nudged by tugs, slipped its moorings and headed out into the English Channel. However, I'm not sure all my recollections were authentic and I wondered if I had really witnessed these very same pomp and ceremony images in countless films.

Our cabin was cramped and basic, but it didn't seem to matter; my sister and I were far too young to appreciate the finer points of cruise liner luxury. We had a porthole which made the room less claustrophobic, less gloomy, but it wasn't a window through which you were granted spectacular views as we were only just above the water line. It had two sets of narrow bunk beds, a hand basin, a radio and a small wardrobe for my mother's striking outfits from Biba. My parents both smoked and the air in the cabin was thick with the tang of my mother's Sobranie cocktails. When her back was turned, I would pilfer a couple of the multi-coloured butts from the overflowing ashtray and experiment with the evil weed in a bathroom down the corridor.

The ship was deemed one class for all, although there was still a passenger hierarchy and the room tariffs corresponded directly with the deck level you were staying on. The expensive suites were located at the top and then decks ran in descending alphabetical order down to G. Most of our deck seemed to be inhabited by families with young children like ourselves.

Oriana's first port of call was the volcanic island of Madeira and here we were allowed off the ship for the first time since leaving Southampton. The weather was disappointingly overcast and humid and we rode in a horse-drawn toboggan as it slid down the steep cobbled streets to the waiting ship below. After taking on supplies, we began the long haul across the Atlantic Ocean to our intended destination some 3,500 miles away.

On the first morning, our parents took us up to enrol in the Oceaneers' Club, where we were left in the capable hands of dedicated P&O staff who made every effort to make our time on board as exciting and creative as possible. We had a base, a collection of interconnecting rooms, with table tennis, table football and air hockey. There were also designated areas for painting and modelling, fancy dress costumes, in fact everything we needed to be entertained for the next three weeks. Children of all ages came and went through those doors, although one girl stood out literally head and shoulders above the rest: she was my nemesis, a formidable opponent, especially when it came to table tennis. Her name was Martine.

During the first few days, the weather was a mixed bag, the ship dipped and rocked and there was a constant stream of casualties running to the toilets. The lady in charge reminded us not to look out of the windows.

'You'll soon have your sea legs. Sea sickness only lasts for a few days.'

My sister spent her time with her best friend Katie. She was the only child of Brenda and Peter (a record producer) who singled my father out as a suitable drinking companion. Peter was handsome in a rugged Viking way and sported a goatee beard. He was loud and brash and it didn't go unnoticed that, like many men on the cruise, Peter couldn't take his eyes or hands off my mother. Many people found him intimidating, but I liked him because he was fiercely patriotic, loved cricket and was always telling me stories about pop stars he'd met or his collection of sports cars. I think mum found him attractive because he was flashy and could tell a story, the complete opposite to my father.

Each morning I waited eagerly for the broadsheet detailing the day's activities to be slipped under the door. There was almost too much choice: treasure hunts, exercise classes, deck quoits, badminton, mini golf, and swimming and diving competitions round the pools every afternoon. I was left to my own devices on the premise that I knew the inherent risks associated with being on a cruise liner in the middle of the ocean. It would have been difficult but not impossible to fall overboard and I think my parents, like many others, adopted the slightly naive view that, as long as I adhered to the laws of the ship, no harm would come to me or my friends…

3

2005

A door slammed.

How long had I been sitting here? Seconds, minutes, an hour? The patchy memories had left me with a sentimental glow and I gathered up the menu card and climbed down. On the landing a cold draught crept round my legs and I made a mental note to check all the window fastenings in the morning. I stopped at Hope's door and checked on her one last time. The small shape curled up in the duvet reminded me of a dormouse hunkering down for winter.

I resisted the urge to lie with her, padded quietly from her room and placed the menu card in a desk drawer. Wearily, I undressed and burrowed under the bed clothes. Within seconds the glowing numbers on the alarm clock blurred.

I was falling.

I screamed.

Seconds later I hit the water.

'Man overboard!' someone shouted.

The water was freezing and the waves, each higher than the last, lapped at my chin. I looked up, there was a figure, a girl watching me. I called out to her...

'Dad, wake up!'

Part of the dream lingered and in a state of panic I tried to save myself.

'Don't let me ...'

'Dad, let me go, you're hurting me! You've got to get up!'

I rubbed my eyes and Hope's impish face appeared.

'I'm sorry. What time is it?'

Hope looked at the clock and counted on her fingers.

'Eleven o'clock.'

My mind prepared an explanation for the headmaster, through a dense fog of tiredness. We can't have slept through the alarm. I sat up as a distant part of my brain flipped a switch and sent a message.

There is no school today. I exhaled loudly, as utter relief coursed through my weary body.

'It's an Inset Day,' I shouted and pinched Hope's cheek a little too roughly.

'Ouch, dad!'

I apologised and lowered my head back into the comfort of the downy pillow as the images of the nightmare gently ebbed away.

Hope jumped onto the bed and rubbed her nose against mine in our ritual Inuit greeting.

'Dad, come on.'

I held her in the crook of my arm.

'It's OK, there's no school today. How about making this old grizzly bear a cup of tea?'

Hope grabbed my arm with more force this time.

'There's someone at the door.'

I kicked off the duvet and dragged myself out of bed. Hope pushed me from behind as I hobbled to the dresser.

'Hurry up!'

I glimpsed my face in the mirror, my sallow skin grimy from my late-night excursion and dark bags sagging under my eyes.

I gathered the front door keys from the table and stood by the window to check my mobile for messages. The weather girl had predicted a cold snap and hailstones drummed hard against the glass. Hope pulled me towards the bedroom door.

'Damn, no bars. OK, let me get some clothes on.'

She pushed and pulled.

'Hurry up, you smelly old bear.'

I reached for my dressing gown and took the stairs two at a time. I smoothed down a lock of hair, tightened the belt and opened the front door. A ferocious gust of wind flung leaves and twigs into the porch and a bony hand brushed mine. I blinked. A small, hooded figure stood in front of me, cradling something in her arms.

'…a cake and a welcome to the village…will be very happy...'

Rain cascaded down her hood, leaving a small puddle around her feet and the rest of her words were lost in the howling wind.

I reached out to accept it.

'Thank you. You are very kind.'

The red tin was warm and I placed it behind me on a shelf overflowing with shoes and trainers.

'I didn't get your name?'

I peered back through the sheets of rain but the path was empty.

Hope appeared by my side.

'Who was it?'

I scratched my head, puzzled.

'I didn't get her name. God I hope she wasn't walking far.'

I sat on the stairs and a scene from a 1970s movie flashed into my head.

Hope tugged my arm.

'What did she want?'

I shook my head to dispel the macabre knife-wielding image of a dwarf in a red raincoat.

'I'm not sure.'

I smiled and ruffled her hair.

'Can you smell that? I think that kind old lady baked us a cake. Come on, I'm hungry and breakfast has arrived.'

I stood up, put my arm protectively around my daughter and closed the front door.

4

The next day the hail and sleet had abated and the silhouettes of trees were framed against a cobalt sky. Yesterday I'd prepared a packed lunch, PE kit and polished shoes. I was trying to be organised but we were still rushing. Every day was a new challenge and part of me lived in the present while another part lived in a perpetual miasma of sorrow. Anna would be my gaping wound that would never heal.

'Shoes on, let's go,' I said irritably.

I watched Hope struggle to fasten a small comb into her hair, her tongue protruding between the gap in her front teeth. We were both suffering from first day nerves and I berated myself for raising my voice.

'Here, let me help.'

I played an imaginary drum roll in the air.

'Look at you, all ready for your new school.'

Hope's arms hung by her sides. She looked awkward and boyish in her new uniform. If Anna had been here, she would have huffed and puffed about the merits of private education, but the village school came highly recommended. I decided not to comment on her slightly menacing appearance and pulled her sweatshirt straight.

'Come on, hat, gloves and coat, it's cold outside.'

The pavement had an icy sheen and soon we were joined by other children, who ran and jumped off walls, the heat from their exertions billowing like dragons' breath from their mouths. Their faces sparkled in the crisp morning air and momentarily their zest for life lifted me, although this morning every bone in my body wanted to crawl back to the warmth and safety of my bed.

It was only a short walk to the school, although as we arrived it was evident the bell had rung. The playground was silent and my words of good luck were rushed as she wriggled free from my awkward embrace and ran in behind a large boy with a satchel.

Late on her first day.

Anna used to admonish me for never being on time for anything. But it was not her voice I heard this morning, but one of my housemasters taking me to task over my end of term report. I was ushered into his musty office heated by an old electric bar fire and the brief meeting ended with familiar words of dissatisfaction.

'More application, less daydreaming. Must do better.'

Things hadn't changed much I mused and pushed my hands deep into the pockets of my overcoat.

I was about to join a column of parents hurrying back to their warm homes when I stopped dead in my tracks. Up ahead a blonde lady disappeared around the corner with a boisterous dog. My scalp tingled in that way when someone walks over your grave. My shoulders slumped.

Anna's dead.

She died three years ago and I cursed silently as painful memories of my failed marriage tumbled into my subconscious. The wind bit into my face and I hitched up my collar and started to walk home. I glanced at a row of small cottages, crammed together like tombstones, their chimneys stained with soot. After a hundred yards the lines of grey stone stopped and there in the next plot stood a cottage with faded pink weatherboards. It reminded me of our dream house, a perfect Hansel and Gretel cottage with low ceilings and oak beams.

It was always bitter-sweet looking back. I remembered how much Anna loathed cruises, she thought they were for the old and infirm, she preferred a little more culture, a little more…je ne sais quoi. She was adamant that a holiday experience should be just that, an experience that allowed you to peer into the soul of a particular place.

I sighed. On this point I totally agreed with her. Now Anna and the house on the green were gone and I felt a vast emptiness, an encroaching black hole that threatened to swallow me up. I reached the front gate in a state of limbo and gripped the icy cold metal tightly trying to divert my melancholy thoughts.

Pull yourself together

Smoke drifted upwards into the sky and I realised that I would need to order coal for a fire. I should build one tonight, Hope would love the campfire camaraderie. A few seconds later I flipped the latch and walked up the path, my feet crunching on the shingle with a renewed sense of purpose.

The cottage was unappealing from the outside. The grey stone was tinged briny green by decades of rainwater, the window frames and soffits were weathered, and there were slates missing from the roof, but it had a porch for wellingtons and coats and a certain feel. More importantly, we enjoyed the novelty of walking to school. I hoped this would be just the tonic we needed, a fresh start, a new life. I knew in time the wounds would heal sufficiently for us to move on. I hung up my coat, walked into the kitchen and put the kettle on.

I decided to rent until we found our feet, until our ship got its bearings. As I got to know the village and all its quirks, I soon became aware that I had stepped back in time; there was no post office or shop within walking distance, the surrounding lanes had no street lights and once the sun set, only the glow of an occasional porch lantern pierced the inky blackness.

We were situated on the edge of the Peak District National Park, the landscape wild and bleak, dotted with forests and quarries, and traversed by endless miles of stone walls. It rose in peaks and troughs from the flat glacial plains of Cheshire and on a clear day, they said you could see the Welsh mountains.

It was very different to the clogged greenbelt we left behind in Surrey, all gated mansions and high streets awash with Starbucks, Carluccio's and Hotel Chocolat. Over the years I had become disillusioned, disinterested in the pot of gold for which everyone was rushing around. A week before we left, I met friends at a local pub, trying to convince them, and perhaps more importantly myself, that I was doing the right thing.

'I've been told they're friendlier up north and the cost of living is lower' I said.

'Why the north?' they all asked.

That was the trillion dollar question.

It's where the pin landed, I told them. Many years ago, I had an old friend who lived nearby and I had a few cherished memories of childless weekends spent walking and drinking in cosy pubs with roaring log fires. Of course, my friends didn't buy it. They sat in judgement, labelled me a turncoat, turning my back on them and all I knew. That night as we headed our separate ways, they told me it wouldn't work out, I'd be back within a year. That night I really thought about staying, but deep down I knew I had to leave, for both our sakes.

In those early days I tried to hide my innermost feelings from my daughter, although underneath my exterior bravado I was scared. Scared of failing, again. Maybe if I had been a little less work obsessed, I would have spotted the warning signs, but I was addicted to my work as a film location manager. It paid well, I travelled extensively and mixed with some great people and some not-so-great stars. The final straw for Anna and I was my involvement in the film Gladiator.

The opening scenes were shot in the UK in woodland near Farnham and for weeks we fed two hundred mud-spattered centurion extras from a small trailer on the edge of a muddy field littered with severed limbs and dead horses. Then the whole circus moved on to a stifling hot Turkey, a hedonistic time that unfortunately would be remembered for the unexpected phone call in the middle of the night from Anna. Shortly afterwards, Oliver Reed died; it was one tragedy after another and I dreaded returning home to face my fate.

I admit my career had become a recreational drug that ultimately led to the ensuing separation that shattered our lives into a thousand pieces. I didn't blame Anna, well, not for the actual split. I was neglecting her needs, mentally and physically, too absorbed in my own world, my own self-importance. I "stopped communicating"; isn't that what the therapists say? I loved my work, but the commitment was total and Anna said it changed me, made me narcissistic and selfish. It took me away from my family for long periods and I regretted that now. I ended up missing everything that was important: birthdays, sports days, school plays, summer ice creams…

The old-fashioned kettle whistled and brought me back to the present. I peered at the empty fire grate. How long was it since I'd built a real fire? Instead of reaching for a herbal tea, I made myself a black coffee, location manager strength coffee, sat at the kitchen table and turned on my laptop. It whirred into life and I watched my inbox gradually fill up with spam. I prodded the delete button vigorously as if this mere physical action would wipe my slate clean.

The therapists said just don't look back, although actually obeying that was another matter entirely. I had already missed too much of Hope's early life and my previous role as the visiting court jester was now curbed by more important paternal responsibilities: father, mother, chef, taxi driver, coach, counsellor and crutch. I searched Google for a local coal merchant and dialled the number. They could deliver today and I made a short grocery list that included firelighters and kindling. We'd have a real fire tonight and eat tea on our laps. It would be the start of a new adventure.

-

It didn't take us long to establish some equilibrium and the days in our new house began to fly by. It was, as feared, a bone-numbingly cold start to winter; Christmas and New Year came and went in a flurry of parties, presents, plummeting temperatures and sledge races. The central heating was a little temperamental and the radiators worked intermittently or not at all. Hope's first school report was satisfactory and it seemed she had settled in well. I ran between pillar and post, chopping logs, shoveling snow and collecting rock salt for the driveway.

As for me, I had a funny feeling it wasn't the last I had seen of the blonde lady with the dog. The menu card languished in a dusty drawer, out of sight, out of mind.

Spring arrived joyously and as the hillsides teemed with spring lambs and Easy by The Commodores drifted through from the kitchen, I sensed our old life beginning to fade into the distance.

-

I was in the lounge reading the Sunday papers when out of the corner of my eye I noticed my daughter leaning against the doorframe, her pixie face framed by curtains of shiny hair. I shivered. For a second I saw Anna standing there in her place. Same stance, same stare. I put the paper down.

'What's up?'

'Mrs Grimes said I had to write a story about a sea journey and draw a picture to go with it. The best ones are going to be judged by a lady who writes children's books.'

I placed my arms behind my head.

'Sounds interesting.'

Hope raised her eyes.

'What am I going to write about? I've never been on a ship, I've only been in a rowing boat.'

My response was heavy with sarcasm.

'You poor deprived child.'

Hope fiddled self-consciously with her hair. She knew not to lay the spoilt child act on me. My features softened.

'You've been on Nelson's ship in London. Do you remember that?'

'You're not being much help and anyway that ship didn't go anywhere.'

'You've been in a speedboat or have you forgotten that as well? Look, you'll just have to use your imagination. I'm sure that's what most of the other children will be doing.'

She pulled a sour face.

'Louisa's been on a cruise.'

'Well she would have…'

Louisa apparently had been born with a silver spoon in her mouth and she had a pony.

A cruise.

It took a second for the penny to drop. I took the stairs two at a time and returned to the dining room, out of breath, clutching a manila folder. Hope looked at me expectantly. I waved the card in the air.

'I found this shortly after we moved in and I've been so busy recently…'

I beckoned her over to the table. Hope eyed me suspiciously.

'What is it?'

'Wait and see.'

I placed it in front of me.

'This ship was called the Oriana.'

She studied the front cover.

'Ori-what?'

'Sit next to me and I'm going to tell you about an adventure I went on.'

Her eyes widened.

'I love adventures.'

I ran my hand over the picture.

'When I was thirteen, my parents took me and my sister on a cruise, and this is the menu from that ship.'

'Is it from a restaurant?'

'More or less.'

She placed her hand on mine.

'Why did you go on a cruise when you're afraid of water?'

My dream resurfaced and it left me feeling puzzled. I wasn't able to put an exact date when I started my aversion to water, I just developed a phobia for it over the years. It was Anna who had taken the kids swimming when they were young, while I never felt comfortable once the water reached my waist. I never liked swimming that much anyway and had never looked for an answer to my irrational fear of drowning.

I tapped my temple.

'Maybe I liked other sports better.'

I sensed her interest as her eyes sparkled.

'Tell me where you went on this ship with a strange name.'

I made an effort to dismiss any feelings of uncertainty because I wasn't sure how good my memory was going to be.

'We sailed across the Atlantic Ocean to the Caribbean. We went almost as far as America. We visited exotic islands like Puerto Rico, St. John's in the Virgin Islands, Antigua and Barbados. You might have heard them mentioned at school.'

'Were the islands beautiful, like in Greece?'

Her first holiday abroad there was the benchmark against which any further places of natural beauty would be measured.

'They were more beautiful. The beaches had pure white sand and hammocks hung between coconut trees, just like in the film Robinson Crusoe.'

'I like that story about the man with one leg, did you go there to make a film?'

'No. I'm not old enough to have worked on those old films and you're getting your stories mixed up. It was Long John Silver who had one leg and he was a pirate.'

Hope mimicked the parrot and it brought a wry smile to my lips.

'Pieces of eight, pieces of eight! Tell me a story about pirates.'

'Sadly I can't, but I'll tell you what I can remember and you can fill in any gaps. Maybe draw one of your special pictures.'

Her drawings were legendary and usually involved a kaleidoscope of vivid and garish colours. Her mother had been artistic and liked painting in watercolours.

Hope picked up the card and as if by magic a small envelope fell out onto the table.

'What's this?'

I registered a look of genuine surprise. It had been dark in the loft, but surely I would have felt something tucked inside. I inspected the padded back cover and found a small slit in the back.

She held the envelope aloft. My brow furrowed.

'Here, let me see.'

A few Polaroids fell onto the table.

She picked one up, scrutinising the faded image. She pursed her lips in mock concentration.

'Who's this?'

A young boy was dressed in a silver waistcoat, lamé trousers and platform shoes, his makeover completed by back combed hair and a hairy chest. I reached for my glasses. My mind struggled with the passage of years and it took me a second to grasp who was in the first picture.

'I guess I'm supposed to be a 70s rock star.'

I cringed. It reminded me of the kids bullying me at school. Shirley Temple they called me.

Hope sniggered. She was obviously embarrassed for me.

'You look funny.'

'Thanks. I'm pretending to be a pop star.'

She reached across me for another photograph. The smell of mint and nettles from her newly washed hair reminded me of Anna and I placed an arm round her shoulder, desperately trying to prevent Anna's memory tainting all our happy moments together.

She looked up at me and smiled.

'I wish I had been on this holiday, it looks fun.'

The next photograph was of a girl in a pinafore dress, a brown mouse and a small child in a top hat.

'It's Alice in Wonderland,' Hope announced proudly.

'And those are great costumes.'

She scrutinised the picture again.

'Who's the girl in the top hat?'

After a few seconds the penny dropped.

'I think that's your Aunty Milly.'

Hope studied my face, looking for some faint facial resemblance. I sucked in my cheeks. I hadn't seen my sister for at least 10 years. We had grown apart and then she emigrated to Australia with her husband and 3 young children. I didn't even know her current address. I sighed, a tinge of sadness in my voice.

'You know, it was a long time ago. We've all changed a lot since then.'

She peered at the third photograph. In the foreground, a young ballerina posed provocatively for the camera, while behind her a line of ballerinas balanced on tiptoe. I had to look twice to be sure and then I began to laugh. She pinched my side playfully.

'What's so funny?'

I pulled away.

'Look closer.'

The ballerinas were dressed in white corsets, although they had muscular legs, and their chins were covered in dark stubble. I pointed to a man with blonde curly hair.

'See that man there? That's your grandad.'

She scrutinised the photograph.

'Why is he dressed as a ballerina?'

'He was in the ship's production of Swan Lake. You see the beautiful girl in the middle? She's the elegant swan, Queen Odette, and the other ballerinas are her swan maidens.'

I could tell by the way she chewed her hair she was confused, so I decided not to burden her with a detailed synopsis of the complicated Russian ballet.

The final photograph was taken at a beachside bar. I peered closely at the suntanned faces sharing a joke. However, Hope soon lost interest in it and her eyes turned back to the menu.

'Let's look at this now.'

I placed the card in front of her and followed her fingers as she traced over the writing as if she was reading Braille. On closer inspection, I noticed the page was covered with barely legible words. I looked over her shoulder.

'Stop, move your hand.'

She looked up at me confused.

'Why?'

I pointed to the bottom of the inside cover.

'Here.'

I nudged her arm.

'Can you read these?'

'Of course I can.'

Hope's eyes were far keener than mine and she began to decipher some of the words.

'Peter, the Captain,' she announced.

Unsure of my facts, I blustered my way through the next few questions.

'Only the special people were invited to sit with the Captain.'

'Was he sitting at your table?'

'No, it's the other way round. You have to be invited to sit at the Captain's Table.'

'And where would we sit?'

'Younger children would eat earlier at the Cat's table. But you were only allowed to drink milk for the entire three weeks.'

I squeezed her shoulders.

'Ha ha, that's funny.'

The last two pages were stuck together.

'Careful don't tear them.'

A tug of war ensued.

'Let me see who else has signed it.'

I delicately pulled the pages apart. Her nose inched closer to the menu card.

'Look, here are more names. Colin Waiter.'

I contained my amusement.

'Yes, you're right, and look, the whole band has signed their names. Oh look, here's a funny line. The first squiggle on the moon. What a strange phrase, I have absolutely no idea what it means.'

Hope didn't either, but she had found something far more interesting. She began to eye me suspiciously.

'This message says: "To gorgeous Paul." That's your name.'

I felt my face blush.

'I wonder who wrote that?'

'I know who wrote it. See here. "Lots of love and kisses from Suzanne."' Hope blew kisses in my direction.

Suzanne.

The name didn't resonate with me even though it appeared I had had an admirer. I found another point of interest further down.

'Look, here's one from someone called Twig.'

Hope giggled.

'That's a funny name! Did he like Twiglets?'

Underneath his name he'd written "And all I've done."

She clapped her hands.

'What did he do?'

'I have no idea. I hope it wasn't anything bad.'

Underneath was his real name.

'See, down here's his name: Robert Tyler.'

Hope stroked the hairs on my arm affectionately. I looked at my watch. It was well past lunchtime and I hadn't prepared anything; however, she seemed engrossed by the children's anecdotes and her voice rose an octave as she read on.

'"To my boyfriend, Paul."'

I cleared my throat.

'It seems I was quite popular.'

She nodded and wagged a finger in my direction.

'You had lots of girlfriends.'

I held my hands up.

'It looks like it, partner.'

She perched on the edge of her seat.

'Do you think there are more photographs somewhere?'

'You never know, maybe grandma has some?'

We continued to study the card and it became clear there were names and addresses from all over the country, from Lancashire and the Peak District in the north, to Essex, Hertfordshire and London in the south. Some passengers had left amusing comments, their quips frozen in time. In my mind I tried to construct a mental picture of the children, but I couldn't, it was just too long ago.

She fidgeted.

'I'm thirsty, can I have a glass of milk?'

She was about to get off her chair when an address at the bottom of a page caught my eye. My hand shook a little as I held onto her arm.

'Hold on.'

I read the address out loud.

'The White House, Sugar Lane, Adlington, near Macclesfield, Cheshire.'

Directly below the address was a six-digit telephone number.

'Is it nearby?' she asked expectantly.

'I'll have to look at a local map, but it might be.'

She frowned and placed her hands under her chin.

'Can we see if we can find the house? Maybe one of your girlfriends lived there?'

I laughed at my daughter's optimism. A world full of innocence, a world where everything was possible. I hadn't considered the idea that one day my teenage past would catch up with me. I felt a strange sensation in my stomach, a mixture of unease and excitement. I perched my daughter on my knee.

'Maybe they do, but there's a good chance the house might not even be there anymore.'

'Please can we try and find it?'

It was time to compromise.

'We can't go today, because, if I'm not mistaken young lady, you have a school project to start, but I promise if all your homework is finished tonight, we'll go and have a look next weekend. Is that a deal?'

She raised her small hands and we high fived.

'A deal.'

After Hope went upstairs, I started to turn things over in my mind. Maybe this foray into my past was a good thing and would help in some way to blot out all the recent grief. I had undergone regular counselling and soon realised there was to be no quick fix. The healing process would be a lengthy one. At the end of each session the therapist would repeat the same words.

'Stop blaming yourself for events you're unable to control.'

I was told to live in the present, but what the hell, as my mother frequently reminded me, I was a curious guy. I walked into the kitchen, my accountability sheet was already pinned to the wall and I ticked off another clean day as I took a ginger beer from the fridge. I took my drink back into the lounge where the photographs and menu card were spread out on the dining table. Come on what harm could it do? It might be fun looking back.

5

At the weekend we set off in search of The White
House. Up ahead, a young rider tried to control a
skittish horse and I braked gradually, giving the
animal a wide berth.

'See how dangerous it is riding on these narrow
lanes?'

Hope was too absorbed in her new role as daring
super-sleuth and my words fell on deaf ears. We
passed The Ship Inn and I reflected that recently
another ship had been at the forefront of my mind and
that perhaps today's journey was some sort of
emotional coping mechanism.

As if reading my thoughts, a breezy westerly
chased the black clouds away and I felt the warmth of
the sun's rays through the glass. I drove out of the
neighbouring village, past the cricket ground with its
freshly painted sightscreens and pavilion, past row
upon row of tiny terraced cottages, until the road
began to wind upwards. I took one hand off the wheel
and stroked Hope's shoulder.

'How's it going navigator?'

Hope gave me a thumbs up. She was clearly
enjoying herself.

The road straightened, we crossed a canal bridge
and Hope waved to a couple on a colourful barge as it
cruised sedately beneath us.

'That looks like fun. Do people live on them?'

I frowned. I'd been on a canal boat holiday in my
student days. In the 1980s we'd travelled from
Oxford to Coventry and back during one of those
endless summer holidays everyone seemed to enjoy

back then. There were eight of us, high on life, unhindered by life's baggage, all dreaming about our futures: that is, until the chemical toilet flooded, I got food poisoning and one of the girls nearly drowned. I teased a smile out for my daughter.

'Some people do. It's cheaper than buying a house, but I bet it's cold in winter.'

For a while we drove parallel to the old railway line, last used in the 1970s. The disused cuttings were now a nature reserve running for miles in both directions and this morning they were dotted with cyclists and walkers.

'Is this the right road?' Hope asked.

'I thought you were navigating?'

She buried her nose in the map.

'I am.'

I glanced down and noticed she was holding the local street map upside down, but I didn't interfere. She grinned back at me.

'I'm not very good with maps am I?'

I turned into Sugar Lane. The road was little more than a single track, dotted with clumps of blooming daffodils, the hedgerows an unkempt fringe on one side. Most of the properties sat away from the road, up along rutted tracks and I soon began to wish I had purchased a Land Rover instead of my rear wheel drive saloon. I drove at a crawl, looking left and right for house names. After five minutes I began to worry that I'd embarked on a wild goose chase.

'Let's hope the house was given its name due to its colour, at least then it should be easy to see.'

Hope pressed her nose tightly up against the passenger window. After passing a farm entrance where cows lolled their heavy heads on a five-bar gate, I pulled into a lay by bordered by high hedgerows. She undid her seat belt.

I pressed her back into her seat.

'Wait.'

'I can't see.'

I pointed over the hedge where an ivy-clad property loomed, the white plaster façade partially visible. I couldn't read the plaque above the porch but I knew it was the right house. She knelt up on her seat. I could feel her whole body tremble with excitement.

'Maybe your girlfriend still lives here.'

I smiled and stroked her hair.

'I don't think so, it was a long time ago. Anyway, we can't just go knocking on the doors of complete strangers, that would be rude.'

A cloud drifted across the sun and finally I was able to read the words etched into the arched lintel.

The White House. 1932.

From the gate, a gravelled path forced its way through the garden, pushing on and around a line of terracotta pots. There was a car on the drive and Hope grabbed my arm.

'We just came to look,' I said

She shrugged her shoulders and sighed.

I looked back at the white villa and memories came flooding back like a tickertape of old film running through a projector. I was sitting in a small kitchen with orange cupboards and Formica work tops. The room smelled of chip fat and my mother was sprinkling brown sugar on steaming bowls of porridge. She had a travel brochure in her hand. My parents enjoyed travelling and the previous year had been to Rio De Janeiro with dad's horse racing friends; however, my sister and I weren't expecting her to announce we were going on a cruise. Now this wasn't your run of the mill holiday down the Nile or to the Mediterranean; it was three weeks aboard the second largest cruise ship in the world as it sailed to the Caribbean. And here, in this house, 200 miles away, a similar family did exactly the same.

I shivered, although I wasn't sure if it was déja vu or a drop in the outside temperature. I felt caught between past and present and my daughter's voice seemed to come from far away.

'Dad! You're daydreaming again.'

A black cloud hovered directly overhead, spots of rain spattered against the windscreen and as I watched them race down the glass, I felt a connection with the house. I was open-minded where fate and providence were concerned and I was of the belief that it was entirely probable that all our lives were interconnected in some way by threads of random chance, imprints that linked us in some invisible way to others. I wound down my window fully and looked at the house. Was that what was happening now?

My daughter gently took my hand as a jay on a nearby fence sang to its mate.

'I'm hungry.'

And with those two simple words, I was humbly brought back to the present.

'Sorry, I was miles away. Put your seat belt on. We'll stop for doughnuts on the way home.'

I knew I was ignoring my own rules on sugar intake, taking the easy route, but before I could change my mind, Hope clapped her hands.

'Yippee! Don't forget to tell grandma about the photographs.'

'Of course I won't.'

I turned the key in the ignition and accelerated up the lane without looking back.

Coincidences?

A tiny part of me wasn't so sure.

Later, after Hope was in bed, I crept along to the spare room-cum-office and switched on my laptop. The WiFi coverage was poor and I waited patiently for the search engine to load. The page eventually appeared and I typed Oriana into the search bar and hit return.

A few minutes later, after clicking on link after link about P and O's modern fleet, I struck gold. Our ship had undertaken her maiden voyage to Sydney in 1960 and there followed a host of colour photographs accompanied by Pathé News-type quotes charting her life cruising the world's oceans. She ceased active service in 1986, when she was sold to a Japanese company and ended up neglected in the port of Osaka after the company that bought her ran out of money. In 1999 she was bought by a Chinese consortium and moved to Shanghai, where she was refitted as a floating tourist attraction. Sadly, the venture wasn't as profitable as the company had wished and she was sold to another Chinese company in Dailan, where she underwent yet more renovations. After being damaged by a storm in 2005 she was eventually moved to a scrap yard in China. I felt a tinge of sadness as I read all this, a colossus of the seas succumbing to the pounding of hammers and welding torches. I re-read the last part of the article.

2005.

My scalp prickled. This year.

What the hell?

The ship and all its memories were no more.

After a quick sandwich break at my desk, I found an interesting article entitled "One Class For All". In the 1950s and 60s, only the rich were able to afford the luxuries of First Class sea travel, while the majority of passengers had to endure a much different experience below decks. In 1973 the ship finally dispensed with First Class travel, thus allowing all fare paying passengers to enjoy the entire ship's facilities.

The screen dimmed and I leaned back in my chair, placed my feet on the desk and closed my eyes. Finding this house had been a peculiar business, being both introspective and energising at the same time, and as I sat in the semi-darkness I decided I wanted to find out more about our cruise to the Caribbean. I reached for my mobile and scrolled down my list of contacts. Frustratingly, the call went to voicemail, so I left a brief message.

In bed, my mind was full of unanswered questions and I tossed and turned as scenes from my past returned and filled my mind; snippets of conversations, laughter and games, children's faces and stolen kisses.

Please let sleep come.

Tonight though, the bed had no boundaries and as my eyelids grew heavy, ghosts from my past crowded into the darkened room.

I was back on the ship.

'Where are the girls?' I asked.

'Playing boring table tennis,' an older boy replied

'Come on let's go and hide in the lifeboats like James Bond,' another said.

'Good idea, we don't need dumb girls do we,' the older one said.

Then I was falling from a great height.

A girl stood at the rail. Why didn't she call for help? The waves lapped at my chin and the girl turned and walked away. Once again I was left alone, a tiny speck in a huge ocean.

6

I woke with a jolt. The bedsheet felt clammy and a fine sheen greased my forehead. I turned to look at the luminous cube beside me.

6am.

I muttered something blasphemous into the darkness and dragged myself out of bed. The floorboards creaked as I padded to the bathroom. The dream seemed so real and images hovered round the edge of my subconscious like ripples on the surface of a lake

Perhaps looking at the old photographs had sparked some form of recovery activity in a far part of my brain? I looked at my reflection in the mirror and bloodshot eyes stared back at me. I poked my furred tongue out and the mirror returned the compliment. I gripped the sink and focused on my breath. I had practised yoga as part of my recovery and I knew how to tune into my prana. The relaxation technique worked and after a few minutes I returned to the sanctuary of my bedroom until it was time to get up.

Like Bob Geldof, I still hated Mondays and this morning a Scandinavian chill filled the air. It made my teeth ache and two pairs of socks offered no protection against the sub-zero temperature. On the way back from school I heard my phone ring and I held a knitted glove between my teeth as I pressed accept.

'Hi Mum,' I mumbled.

'You sound like you have cold.'

'No, a mouth full of glove. I've just dropped Hope at school.'

'Oh I see. How is my granddaughter?'

I held the phone against my shoulder as I replaced my glove.

'She's fine.'

'And how are you coping?'

'A few teething problems but we're both good thanks.'

I knew what was coming and I prepared myself.

The phone crackled.

'Can you hear me?'

'Yes I can, the signal's back now.'

'My bag is packed, all you need to do is pick up the...'

The signal drifted.

'Mum, listen...'

'It must be difficult being a single parent and what with you suddenly uprooting...'

'Mum...'

We only occasionally spoke about my past addictions.

'...I'm allowed to be concerned aren't I?'

I tried to deflect her worries.

'Of course you are, but as I explained before, I feel this uprooting, call it what you want, change, is our best chance to move on.'

A brief silence followed, which meant my point had been registered although probably not agreed with.

'Well, does this country life suit you?'

I waved to a neighbour.

'Yes, it's beautiful up here, in a wild rugged way.'

I opened the gate cradling the phone on my shoulder, waiting for her questions to move into more personal areas.

'And have you thought about work? You can't afford to retire.'

I sighed.

Here it comes.

'Hold on, I'm home now.'

I opened the front door and kicked it shut with my heel.

My mother and I had always been close, maybe too close. Over the last few years she had helped me through the darkest of times, although sometimes she clearly forgot I was an adult. I think this maternal allegiance stemmed from our early relationship. I remembered her showing me photographs of fashion shoots and drinks parties in the swinging 1960s where I was being mollycoddled by her glamorous friends: the endearing boy who all the girls wanted to mother.

Her little black book landed me my first break in the film industry, although I wished she had spent more time on my early development: important intrinsic values had not been passed on to me in her quest for self-gratification. Luckily, I grew up to be a popular young man, however those same self-destructive traits always lurked close to the surface. When Anna and I were married, my behaviour at social gatherings was inexcusable; on a scale of 1–10 it was probably an eleven. Sometimes I didn't give a fuck, I would rather sneak off to the gents and do a line of coke. The more sensitive the social situation, the more I was expected to behave like the perfect husband, the more I behaved like a complete prick. I couldn't have displayed less empathy if I'd suffered from Asperger's, though I didn't have any such legitimate excuse.

My mother's probing continued as I hung my coat up.

'Don't avoid the subject, you're a man with needs like any other.'

I felt my hackles rise. I bit my lip.

'Mum, leave it.'

'You know darling, it's like riding a bike, you need to get back in the saddle as quickly as possible. It's not healthy to be on your own for too long, just look at what it did to your father.'

I took a deep breath and exhaled slowly though my mouth. In. Out.

'Everything is very new up here.'

I could almost hear the cogs turning inside her head.

How did she know?

'You've met someone. I can sense it.'

'It's early days' I said breezily.

-

We had been the only two parents waiting by the gate. She leaned casually against the dry stone wall, her scruffy jeans tucked into Timberland boots, a baseball cap pulled down tight over wisps of blonde hair. Her resemblance to Anna was uncanny. Then she was standing next to me and a very pleasant waft of something fresh and zingy drifted my way.

She smiled at me and I tried to work out how old she was.

'Do you think we've been set up? Feels a bit like dating corner doesn't it?' she said.

I looked around for some moral support but we were alone.

'Yes it does…I mean no…'

Her eye contact was intense.

'I've always wanted to meet a film star.'

I looked puzzled and kicked a stone into the road. She clearly had mistaken me for someone else. Then it clicked.

'Robyn's mum?'

'Spot on. My name's Amber.'

She removed a frosty mitten and before we shook, I noticed how incredibly smooth and perfectly manicured her hands were. It was a piece of grooming I was particularly obsessive about. My mother called it my five-fingered OCD. Amber's mittens dangled on elastic below her hands and my eyes lingered a little too long at the slight absurdity of her attire.

She sensed my eyes on her hands and smiled. It knocked me sideways.

She shrugged.

'Blame my parents.'

I laughed nervously, but I was unsure if she thought I was laughing with her or at her. It wasn't a great start.

'You know I'm not a...'

She averted her eyes in mock disappointment.

'I know, it's a shame. I thought it might be a little far-fetched up here in sleepy hollow.'

I blustered on, inspecting my own hands in an overly self-conscious way.

'Hope doesn't quite understand the difference between actors and crew and has an embarrassing habit of misleading people. A few years ago, she told everyone I had a Porsche!'

Amber gave me a sympathetic look that suggested she understood children's made up fantasies, although I sensed she would have quite liked it if it had been true. On closer inspection her face was line free and I reckoned she was a few years younger than me.

I found the combination of perfect hands and her understated confidence very attractive and when she laughed her whole face lit up like Princess Diana's used to. The powerful flow of energy between us meant I had to avert my gaze and my trance-like state was only broken by children's voices in the playground. I waved to Hope and at the same time I realised I hadn't introduced myself properly.

'I'm Paul, but you probably know that already.'

Her pale blue eyes bored into mine, as if everything I said was vitally important. She nudged my arm.

'Look, here they come.'

'Why are the girls so late?' I asked.

'It's the poster competition for healthy eating. They've been put forward as finalists. You must have seen Hope's latest picture? Everyone's talking about it.'

I metaphorically kicked myself. Damn. Of course I had.

-

Mum coughed and derailed my reverie.

'Burgers are banned, veggies are grand!' I said under my breath.

'Sorry.'

'Nothing, just a catchy strapline I can't get out of my head.'

My mother cleared her throat. She knew exactly which buttons to push.

'So, what does she look like?'

She knew my choice of women was predictable, there was no hiding the fact.

'There is a slight resemblance to Anna,' I said, then paused. Silence.

Happy now?

'Oh, and she likes pizza,' I added as an afterthought.

Mum and Anna never saw eye to eye. Anna with her winning smile and pure white teeth, Anna always immaculate with her blonde hair pulled tight in a ponytail. However, getting caught with Charles in the rugby club toilets was reckless and careless. I found out later that they'd been meeting in secret for ages. I was angry and full of self-remorse, but none of our friends seemed remotely surprised. Twelve years of marriage down the swanny.

I knew I wasn't blameless, although it was a hollow victory tinged with acrimony. Charles and I were best friends and when I was home we stood together watching the 1st Fifteen eating bacon rolls, ketchup dripping down our chins, while the lads scrummed and scrimmaged in the mud. We attended the same dinner parties, the rugby club ball; for God's sake, we almost went on holiday together! It all happened so quickly, it was like our past had never existed. It was like Hope and I had never existed.

Before the courtroom battles, lies and lawyers' bills could begin, Anna lost control of her car on a dangerous hairpin as she drove back from her mother's villa in the south of France. I found out later she was returning to end our marriage properly.

Her body was flown back and the funeral was a blur. It was heart-wrenching and surreal at the same time, fingers were pointed and there were recriminations and accusations from both sides. The whole thing was a fucking mess. After the funeral and the legal formalities were completed, I made a promise to Hope that one day we would make a fresh start, a new beginning. Charles and I hadn't spoken since that day at the church, when her casket blanketed with red roses was lowered into the freshly dug grave.

I held the phone at arm's length and shook an imaginary fist as my mother continued to prattle on.

'Well, I hope this young lady can raise your spirits darling.'

Even though we were hundreds of miles apart I imagined my mother's rosebud lips, enjoying her play on words.

I cut in.

'The reason I called yesterday was because I've got something interesting to tell you.'

'Really?'

'Do you remember that old chest, the one with my initials on it?'

'I do.'

'I found something in it.'

'And what might this something be?'

'A menu from the Oriana.'

'A menu! It's of little value I suspect. Your father threw so much stuff away at the time of the divorce I could have killed him.'

'Well initially, that's what I thought, and then I discovered names and addresses on it.'

'Traces of our past do have a habit of popping up from time to time and biting us on the behind.'

'There was something in it. An envelope.'

I heard her laugh.

'Money?'

'Photographs.'

My mother sounded indifferent to the news.

'Of the cruise, I presume.'

I didn't speak, I played her at her own game. She hated long-drawn-out silences.

'How extraordinary. Who's in them?'

'Me as a 70s popstar.'

There was a shift in the tone of her voice, a level of interest not there minutes before.

'Well, I deserve some credit for that. I beg, stole and borrowed for that outfit.'

I walked upstairs to my office where the photographs were laid out on my desk.

'There's one of Milly as the Mad Hatter and a hilarious one of dad as a ballerina. How old was I back then?'

'Let me think. It was '74 so that would make you about thirteen. I bet you had a good laugh, there will never be another production of Swan Lake to match it. The ballet was the highlight of the cruise and had been choreographed by a professional dancer. She was no more than twenty and those men used to tease her something rotten during rehearsals. I wouldn't be surprised if she had to put one or two of her hirsute entourage in their place, especially Peter and your father, the dirty buggers.'

'In one photo there's a group of you at a beach bar.'

My mother whistled.

'How delightful. I wish I was there now.'

'The picture is quite faded. You and dad are looking, how shall I put it politely, very merry.'

She paused and I heard papers shuffled.

'God, don't remind me, your father was always pissed. I've never seen anyone down banana daiquiris like him. They were all rolling drunk when they did the ballet. Sorry to go on, but that poor girl deserved a medal.'

I studied the photograph: something wasn't quite right. It was slightly smaller than the others and I ran a finger along the edge. It was uneven, like it had been cut.

'Are you still there?'

'Sorry Paul, I was thinking. It was a long time ago. Oh yes, I remember now. We were in Barbados. I believe it was just before we headed home. We got taxis to Cobblers Cove, an exclusive hideaway on the coast. We only had a few hours there because we had to be back at the ship by dusk.'

'Where were we?'

'God, don't ask me. I presume you were playing on a nearby beach. We were so relaxed about our parental responsibilities, it's quite shocking thinking about it now. Anyone could have snatched you and we wouldn't have known for hours.'

Her soothing voice soon whisked me off to an idyllic Caribbean beach.

'We were sitting on the terrace with Peter and Brenda Barfield, they had a daughter called Katie, do you remember? I think there was another couple from Cambridge, whose names were…no I can't remember. Peter was a real smoothy, a bit of a poser really. He used to know Herb Alpert and he took us to Ronnie Scott's a couple of times when we got back. Those were the days.'

'I remember Peter.'

He was a man you definitely wouldn't forget.

'You formed a gang. You called it the E deck gang. You and your friends were like sprites stalking the adult world.'

'The E deck gang, I like that.'

'You had some fun. You mischievous lot kept us on our toes.'

I ran my finger over the menu card.

'It sounded like we had the run of the ship. Can you remember any of the children's names?'

'Names? Gosh, it was a long time ago. I do remember you were best friends with a thin boy who reminded me of "Stig of the Dump" because he always looked like he needed a decent bath. His nickname was Twig. He was double-jointed and used to make the girls scream when he pulled his thumb back to touch his wrist. As for you young man, I don't know what you had back then but we should have bottled it. Those girls were like bees round a honey pot.'

I laughed nervously at the metaphor.

'So it seems. Do you have any more photographs?'

'I'll have a look, but I'm not promising I'll find anything. There might be some in the boxes lurking at the back of the garage. To be perfectly honest, I'm surprised those photographs turned up.'

I checked my watch. I had some mail to go through.

'Only if you get time.'

'You could ask your father, he may have some tucked away somewhere. You know I haven't seen him in years, he's so wrapped up in his own life now.'

I sighed.

'He'll never change.'

'You're right. I'm so glad you're not like him.'

It was common knowledge that my father's behaviour during the cruise had been shameful. I had been told Peter and my father were accused of shooting at the seabirds perched on the funnel. They were brought before the Chief Officer and banned from clay pigeon shooting for the rest of the cruise. Thinking back now, many of their antics were straight out of a Carry On film.

'Don't remind me, thank God I didn't get his genes.'

I heard the chink of a china cup on a saucer and when she spoke her voice had an urgency to it.

'You'd go off for hours on end, to where, we never knew. It made your father really mad, but I defended you to the hilt. I told him you were just a young boy having fun.'

For a moment I felt something rise to the surface. I hadn't expected the conversation to go in this direction and I instinctively wanted to know more.

'I was only thirteen…'

Down the phone I heard a doorbell ring.

'Look, I've got to go, someone's at the door. We'll speak soon. Look after my favourite grandchild and if I find any more photographs, I'll call you.'

The call ended abruptly without our customary "love you".

Her latest revelation had distracted me and as I toyed with a model sports car, driving it along my desk, I thumped the table with my fist and thought, bugger, I forgot to ask if any of their friends lived in the North West.

7

'Now the hamster's dead, can we get a dog?'

My daughter had inherited her mother's wily negotiating skills and in hindsight I succumbed far too easily to Hope's demand for a puppy. I suppose I wanted to be a father who made all her dreams come true and I dutifully phoned round the local rescue centres. After a few calls I hit the jackpot and drove to Marple in a state of excitement. When the puppy appeared cradled in the handler's arms my heart was won and the decision to keep her instantaneous.

She was the colour of ripe wheat with a white tip on her tail; how could anyone refuse to foster this gorgeous, silky doe-eyed creature? I knew Hope was going to fall in love with this six-week bundle of joy and I kept my fingers crossed the vetting procedure would go smoothly.

Amber insisted that, as she knew the area, she come with me on collection day. How could I refuse? We had been spending more and more time together and slowly but surely she was wearing down my emotional defences. I remembered our first date. I was of course my usual impatient self and immediately wanted to know everything about her, so that it was only her inimitable sensitivity that slowed me down and prevented me spoiling our first afternoon together. The lingering taste of cherry lip gloss was the icing on the cake.

She had studied criminal psychology at Manchester University before setting up her own recruitment company called Concierge. She joked that her knowledge about profiling and assessment of offenders was particularly useful when it came to interviewing potential candidates in her private life.

In between mouthfuls of dough balls smothered in pungent garlic butter, Amber explained she suffered from bouts of cabin fever, brought on by spending too much time in a small room off her bedroom. In this paper-strewn alcove, she held late night telephone interviews and scrutinised CVs. It all sounded very claustrophobic and stressful, but she spoke candidly about juggling work and parenting, so I understood why she chose to spend her free time mostly on the fells with her dog.

'Working for yourself is an uphill battle, one step forward two steps back,' she admitted with a familiar shake of her ponytail. I could see few chinks in her armour as I watched her pick at her pizza, eating only the middle and leaving the crust. Underneath the white teeth and manicured hands, I saw a woman fiercely driven to succeed.

We were studying the dessert menus when her voice faltered. She'd got pregnant. They were both still at University. The news had triggered a multitude of raw emotions: had she found the right man? Did she want to spend the rest of her life with him? She didn't want to end up with someone she felt obliged to stay with because of an unplanned pregnancy, it wasn't in her DNA. In the end, after weeks of soul-searching, she decided to keep the baby and end the relationship.

They agreed on an amicable arrangement that allowed Robyn to spend alternate weekends with her biological father. Amber went on to pass her degree after deferring for a year, although as our date progressed, I began to appreciate that, like me, she was papering over the cracks and the healing process was going to take much longer than she expected.

We shared a tiramisu and our conversation turned to the mums and dads we met at the school gates. There was the mysterious woman in a black Range Rover, the horse breeder, the midwife, the policeman and the quarry manager who liked to tinker with explosives. Once started on the oddballs, the gloating egotists and the downright weird and wonderful, we were unstoppable, dissecting their lives with a fine toothcomb and cackling like two old crones.

It wasn't long before we were huddled like conspirators over our cappuccinos, the focus of our attention the policeman who was making a nuisance of himself by checking people's tax discs after dark. After a second coffee, I paid the bill and we hailed a taxi. I contemplated telling her about the menu card but it seemed of little consequence as I relaxed with her in the back of the cab. I had been relieved she had not quizzed me about my penchant for ginger beer as I knew it was something I needed to discuss, but just not now.

Our afternoon had been like a walk in an orange grove with the sun on your back: her laughter, her honesty, her self-confidence…and her fragrance! There, I'd said it, I was falling and falling fast. She liked animals. Tick. She didn't suffer fools gladly. Tick. Her warped sense of humour was similar to mine. Tick. And she liked the dimple on my chin that she said made me look cute. Tick. Like a good pull on a cigarette, I felt the first signs of addiction.

With the new puppy safely tucked up in the laundry room, I set off to collect Hope from school. Anna always said I was useless with secrets, but on this occasion I managed to contain my own excitement: my lips remained firmly sealed.

Hope swung from my hand, her feet leaving the ground at regular intervals.

'Are we seeing Robyn tonight?'

'Not tonight. It's good for you two to have a break from each other. You know, sometimes I get the impression you'd like to live with Amber instead of me!'

Hope skipped off in front.

'Maybe.'

We stumbled into the porch, lunchboxes, bags and shoes flying in all directions.

'I'm going to watch TV,' Hope announced.

'Whoa! Hang on a minute young lady. Before you disappear, I have a little surprise for you.'

Hope stopped at the foot of the stairs.

'What sort of surprise?'

'Guess.'

She frowned.

'Another hamster.'

I took her hand.

'Wrong. Come with me.'

We stood in front of the utility room and right on cue the puppy scratched at the door.

'Do you hear that?'

She hopped from one foot to the other.

'I can!'

I mimed a theatrical drum roll and opened the door with a flourish. The puppy, no bigger than a rabbit, gamboled out to greet us, running round our legs, wagging its tail energetically. I leant against the door jamb seduced by the look of rapture on Hope's face as she cavorted with this small bundle of blonde fur. We named her Lottie.

-

'What's that for?' Hope asked when she saw me return home one day with a wooden, stair gate.

'Well rather than shutting Lottie in her room, I suggest we erect this barrier, so she can still see us but can't jump out.'

'Cool, let's put it up.'

For a while the stair gate was a roaring success, until one day Lottie appeared in the hallway and made a puddle on the carpet.

The puppy was under my feet clawing at my shoelaces and I shuffled towards the kitchen where I found the barrier to be in place. The two of us stood side by side and scratched our heads.

I reigned in my anger.

'Tell me the truth. Did you let her out?'

She lowered her eyes.

'No. I didn't,' she whispered.

Lottie, bored with my laces, headed for the mesh gate. To our astonishment our canine Houdini wriggled through an invisible tear and bounded down the hall. We both went to grab her, missed and collapsed in a heap. I glanced at Hope's glowing face as we rolled about on the floor. She was growing up fast and for the first time I was struck by a terrible fear. How could I protect her from all the angst in the world? It was an impossible undertaking. I kissed her on the forehead and immediately her eyes welled up.

'I've been thinking about Mummy.'

I placed my arms round her.

'Don't be sad. Mummy is up there watching everything we do. She would be so happy you had a new puppy.'

She wiped her eyes and a goofy smile spread across her face.

'Good. And I will make Lottie the best-behaved dog in the world.'

She sat with the puppy in her lap and I sensed another question.

'You were shouting in your sleep. Were you dreaming about Mummy?'

The bad dreams continued to haunt me and I smiled weakly.

'Yes. I dream about Mummy all the time.'

She raised her eyebrows.

'Good, so do I.'

A heavy weight lay in the pit of my stomach. It was guilt. The disturbing truth was that Anna wasn't the main focus of my dreams anymore.

I put Hope to bed and retired to my office along the landing. While I waited for my laptop to boot up, I glanced at a digital photo-frame portraying images from my film days. One of the photographs was taken in Tunisia, where we were shooting The Mummy. I was precariously balanced on Jimmy the Grip's shoulders, a scarf wrapped round my head like Lawrence of Arabia. My skin was the colour of mahogany and God I was skinny; I looked like a crazed action hero on speed. I remembered how much Anna hated that photograph and now I knew why. She momentarily caught a glimpse of my dark side.

The website loaded and the screen cast a blue glow over the desk. The advert read:

Luxurious 17th Century lodge on the shores of Lake Windermere with prime waterside views. Location; Limefitt Park near Ambleside. Two bedrooms, shower room on ground floor. Small kitchenette and a real log fire.

There was no hot tub. Good, I hated hot tubs, and read on.

The house was secluded and had unrivalled views of the lake and surrounding fells. Undoubtedly it was a potentially romantic venue, I thought smugly. I clicked on images of happy couples enjoying the stunning views from the house.

There had been a significant shift in my feelings for Amber of late and I started to imagine what it would be like to hold her and feel her naked skin against mine. Having recently been consumed by so much bitterness and grief, and the burden of responsibility for my daughter, I began to realise how my own needs had been put on hold. Now it seemed, with Amber bringing some emotional stability, I felt my smouldering libido gradually returning.

More interior images appeared. The lodge had a large fireplace and comfy sofas. A wooden stairway led upwards to a galleried mezzanine floor and the master bedroom. On the ground floor towards the rear was a small kitchenette area and a smaller twin-bedded room. I hurriedly checked on its availability.

The weekend I had in mind was free and more importantly the property was pet friendly. Lottie was too young to take but I knew Amber found it difficult to leave Monty if she went away. All I needed to do was find a babysitter for Hope and the puppy. I reached for my wallet and as the cursor hovered over the "Book Now" button, I hesitated and a cloud of uncertainty descended like a black cloak.

I was out of practice; seduction was something I'd never had to work at, unlike my friends who seemed to tackle the subject like some sort of army exercise. When Anna and I first hooked up, she wondered if I had ever chatted anyone up in my entire life. I had been consistently bad at recognising signs of female desire, so what if I had misread those same signals now? What if she saw this romantic overture purely as an attempt to get her into bed?

I sighed.

And there we had it, man's deep-rooted angst. Rejection.

I sipped my ginger ale. Look at me, I was like a nervous schoolkid. What had happened to the Lothario of 1974, the boy who had all the girls queuing up for his attentions? I clicked on the contact details and picked up the phone.

8

Two weeks later.

It was gone ten when we returned to the house by the
lake after an enchanting evening at a local restaurant.
Amber immediately sensed something was wrong.
Monty had not touched his food and when we let him
out, he ran down to the lake like a dog possessed.
Something or someone had spooked him and Amber
made me search every room before we went to bed.
We both commented afterwards that, even with the
roaring fire, it never felt particularly warm upstairs, it
felt like a window had been left open, but I checked
them all and they were definitely shut tight.

Amber tried to cajole Monty upstairs but he
wouldn't budge and every so often he'd express his
disapproval by a long-drawn-out whine from the
bottom of the stairs. We eventually fell asleep, but it
wasn't long before I was woken by Monty growling.
His snarling forced me out of my dream and even
though not fully awake, I sensed we were not alone.
A wraith like figure hovered on the stairs and pointed
an outstretched finger towards me. Then she or he
just melted away.

In the morning we took Monty and went for a long
hillside walk. I wanted to tell Amber about the figure
I thought I had seen on the stairs, although every time
she mentioned the dog's strange behaviour, I
clammed up. Right or wrong, I didn't think it was the
right moment to go digging up my past.

That evening we had a power cut and while I
searched for a box of candles I stumbled across a

battered and bruised visitor's book in a desk drawer. I lit an oil lamp and while Amber and Monty curled up on the sofa together, I began to read the entries. I flipped back to this time last year and found an entry left by a young couple.

My eyes widened.

I hurriedly turned back another 12 months, my eyes searching for the same date.

I clapped a hand to my mouth as a small cry almost escaped from my lips. There it was again.

I stared into the fire.

Did I believe in ghosts?

A log hissed and spat a burning ember onto the rug as if it disapproved of my idle thoughts. Amber stirred and the blanket I had draped over her slipped to the floor. I turned and smiled.

'Come on, it's late, I'll let Monty out.'

Amber held out her hand and I edged across the floor towards the sofa. Monty jumped off and I curled up with her, intertwined in each other's arms. I clung to her like a child clings to his mother and as nagging doubts about my past resurfaced, she nuzzled my face and neck, with lips that tasted of peaty whisky. We remained in this blissful state until the fire had almost burnt itself out, although I couldn't shake the feeling that something otherworldly, beyond my understanding, was happening to me.

-

A few days after our return I delved into the history of properties in Ambleside. It was a popular tourist destination and I scrolled down endless entries for walking holidays, mini-breaks and local dignitaries opening gastro pubs and boutique hotels. I had almost given up on my search when a headline right at the bottom of the page jumped out at me: *Teenager Goes Missing.* The date was 1971.

It appeared a young girl had gone missing from a nearby farmhouse. Police divers never found her body and it was feared she had drowned in a nearby lake. The mere mention of a drowning brought back my own inexplicable fears of a watery grave. Was I reading too much into my recent night terrors, or was I simply being punished for being a poor husband and father? I closed the laptop and in the eerie silence that followed, I heard my mother reciting her favourite proverb again.

Curiosity killed the cat.

I desperately tried to dismiss any feelings of unease, but the truth was that all my recent insecurities and fears seemed in some way to be linked to my discovery in the loft. Tonight, as if they had strange magnetic powers, I placed the menu card and the photographs onto the kitchen table and willed my subconscious to remember some small detail, something that may have caused my world to tilt so significantly. I felt the heat from the Aga on my back and snippets of memory came back: a bustling fish market, a daytrip to a sugar cane plantation where barefoot bajans shinned up the trunks of coconut trees, a visit to Nelson's Shipyard in Antigua where I straddled the black barrel of a large cannon that poked out across the harbour and I heard music, a familiar song.

Seasons in the Sun.

There was no order to this sequence of random images and I believed they were just memories from existing photographs I had seen countless times before. We criss-crossed oceans and seas, visited breathtakingly beautiful islands and all I was left with was a handful of family snaps. It was as though my mind had wiped my hard drive clean.

Lottie lay at my feet. I felt her stir.

'Come on girl, out you go.'

Lottie yawned and reluctantly headed for the back door.

'Be good girl.'

An owl hooted in the woods and she sniffed the air, before she did her business under a tree. It had been cathartic getting the dog and Hope had surprised me by embracing not only the playtimes but the daily responsibilities that went with owning a pet. She was growing up fast and I would soon have to have the chat about her becoming a woman. I was not looking forward to it one bit and secretly hoped Amber could give me some guidance. I let Lottie back in and ruffled her ears.

'I hope the dreams don't come tonight girl.'

She cocked her head from side to side, listening to the timbre in my voice. I felt her wet nose against my hand and decided to break one of my own house rules.

'You can sleep with me tonight.'

She seemed pleased with this change of routine and followed me jauntily up the stairs. She was already curled up on the bed as I slipped beneath the duvet.

We had joy,
We had fun,
We had seasons in the sun...

I switched off the light, while the song played on repeat in my head.

In the morning, after an uneventful night, I decided it was time to open up to Amber about my past. My phone chirped at me from the dresser. She had got my message and would be round after school pick-up. I smiled apprehensively and killed time with domestic chores and some financial paperwork. When Amber arrived in her battered Audi, the sun was a hazy orange ball and the afternoon was slipping away. After she'd said hello to Hope, I grabbed a jug of homemade lemonade and two glasses and we walked through to the garden.

'Where's Robyn?' I whispered as I put the tray down on a small round table.

'At home with my mum. She wanted to take her shopping.'

She grabbed my hand.

'What's up? Is it Hope? Lottie?'

I looked back towards the house and lowered my voice.

'No. There's something I need to get off my chest.'

Amber unzipped her gilet.

'Well I'm not going anywhere.'

Only when I'd finished my entire heartrending story did she speak.

'God. I was really worried when you said you had something important to tell me.'

Her features softened.

'I had no idea you had been through so much heartache. Well, we've both been knocked about a bit, haven't we?'

I felt a rush of guilt.

'I should have told you about Anna. I feel like I've been hiding things from you.'

Amber leant forward and took my hands in hers.

'I totally understand why you didn't.'

I rolled my shoulders and the tension eased. It always felt better sharing. I took a deep breath.

'All I really want is a little peace for me and Hope. Do you think that's too much to ask?'

My hand shook a little as I poured more lemonade.

'Do you think I'm having a breakdown?'

Amber laughed gently, quietly. Empathy was something that came very naturally to her.

'No, but you're under a lot of pressure. It's stressful and tiring being a lone parent and, well, with all that's gone before, I'm surprised how well you're coping.'

I looked away.

'Thanks for the sympathy vote.'

Then I gathered myself.

'Tell me honestly, what do you think about these dreams I keep having?'

Amber inspected her nails; her cuticles were perfect, as usual.

She always gave a question a lot of thought before answering and I liked that.

'Our brains are very complicated organs. It could just be your mind trying to come to terms with what happened to Anna, or something deeper rooted from your past.'

I tried not to sound over-dramatic.

'Something deeper rooted sounds ominous.'

Ambers eyes narrowed and I sensed her mood change.

'Or perhaps your family has a dark secret.'

I shrugged my shoulders dismissively.

'A dark secret! That's a clichéd statement if ever I heard one.'

Amber looked apologetic.

'I don't have a crystal ball, but I sense there may be more to this story than just teenage crushes.'

A nervous tick started in the corner of my left eye, a sure sign I was stressed.

'Curiosity killed the cat,' I whispered

'Sorry, what did you say?'

'Nothing, just a stupid proverb my mother used to recite when I was up to no good.'

I rubbed my temples as I paced up and down.

'I thought it might be a bit of fun taking Hope to find that house but now I'm beginning to regret it. Maybe I should forget this whole wild goose chase.'

Amber held up her hand.

'Not so fast. Doesn't a tiny part of you want to find out if this family really did live there? Maybe pour some light on this girl you're dreaming about?'

I sat down heavily.

Amber's eyes glowed with excitement.

'This is the stuff films are made of. Come on, it's not that long ago really and some of these farming communities go back generations. I bet someone can come up with some answers.'

I stared long and hard at her clear blue eyes.

'You really think it would help?'

She fixed me with a steely stare.

'Yes I do.'

I grunted.

Amber sipped her lemonade.

'This is lovely by the way.'

She stretched sensuously like a cat and I watched, fascinated, as her limbs curled and uncurled. My mind drifted back to the Lakes and I remembered her body lit by the soft glow of the candles, her face thrown back in exquisite pleasure as we made love for the first time.

Without any warning, the familiar ache of desire returned and I crossed my legs and did my best to ignore the surge of libido.

I tapped my nose with a finger.

'It's my mother's secret recipe.'

'You seem to be very close to her.'

I laughed nervously.

'I suppose I am. I never got on with my father and I spent a lot of time with her when I was younger. She's a very confident women, however, she can be a little controlling. In fact, in some ways she reminds me of you.'

Amber frowned.

'Thanks a bunch!'

'Just little things, I don't know what I'm saying really.'

'Yes you do, come on when do I...'

'When you're being bossy, like now.'

'Oh! And I suppose she knows about me then?'

'I told her I have a friend, that's all.'

'What exactly have you told her?'

'All good things, I promise.'

Amber stepped away from my embrace and frowned.

'There is one thing about all this that bothers me.'

I stepped back, surprised by Amber's harsher tone.

'What's that?'

'Your age. How old were you in 1974, thirteen?
Weren't you quite young to, how can I put this
politely, be putting it about?'

I crossed my arms defensively.

'I don't know if that's exactly the right phrase to
use for puppy love.'

Amber raised an eyebrow.

'I was seventeen when I first slept with someone,
but you were just thirteen.'

My stomach churned and I looked sheepishly at
the ground.

'We were both 14, I think,' I muttered under my
breath.

Amber clicked her fingers bringing me out of my
reverie.

'Can you go and get the menu card?'

'See, you're doing it now.'

'What?'

'Being bossy.'

I smiled, disappeared into the kitchen and returned
with the menu card. We sat side by side on a bench,
the wooden slats still warm from the sun, while
Amber donned her reading glasses and scrutinised the
contents. It was like she was valuing a precious
manuscript from Sotheby's. Eventually she looked
up.

'"To my gorgeous boyfriend," well, you weren't
making it up then.'

I laughed half-heartedly and shrugged a shoulder
nonchalantly.

'You're only thirteen and you have a posse of
young girls chasing you round the decks of this ship.
Surely you can remember if something untoward
happened. Try this. Imagine you're with them now,

try and go back to somewhere familiar, maybe a place on the ship where you all used to meet.'

I closed my eyes. I really tried to concentrate but my mind drew a blank.

'I can't remember anything, zippo.'

'Well, apart from the one who beat you at table tennis.'

Amber shook her head and sighed. I chewed my lip.

'Why are you looking at me like that?'

'I don't know, I'm just flabbergasted by your allure at such a young age.'

'You're pulling that face again.'

'To tell you the truth, I'm trying to imagine all you boys being beaten by a girl at table tennis. How did you live with yourselves?'

'From what I remember she had a very tricky serve.'

'Ah, see, you remembered her serve. Now let's be serious for a moment.'

'You're going to profile me aren't you? You think I'm unhinged…'

Amber pushed her glasses down her nose and peered at me in a quizzical fashion.

'Yes young man, your behaviour does seem a little irrational.'

I looked closely at her face and for the first time I sensed her concern was genuine.

'I want to help.'

I shook my head.

'Why? You've got enough on your plate without this.'

She folded her arms across her chest.

'Because a.) I seem to be smitten with you, and b.) my gorgeous film man, solving puzzles is what I do best.'

Minutes passed while Amber resumed her study of the menu card. Eventually she looked up.

'This is astonishing. You really have to find out who lived in that house.'

I threw my arms into the air.

'What do you suggest? We go and knock on the front door? The property could have changed hands many times since 1974. My own family moved half a dozen times in just ten years.'

Amber pointed a pencil at me.

'Fair point. But if they don't, there are parish records, electoral registers etc...'

'Parish records! Come on, you're taking this too far. This was supposed to be a bit of fun, not the Spanish fucking inquisition.'

There was a glint in her eye.

'Every family has secrets, even yours. Can I have a top up?'

Amber raised her hand.

'Maybe your mother knows something.'

I shrugged my shoulders. Maybe she did?

We both said nothing for quite a while.

'Shall we go in?' I said.

'Can I stay for tea? Mum and Robyn won't be back for ages.'

Amber was nothing but persistent and once inside I dutifully left another message on my mother's voice mail.

Ten minutes later my phone rang.

'I got your message. Are you all OK?'

'Yes, we're all fine.'

We made small talk for a while, the trials and tribulations of puppy training, and I mentioned a recent book I'd read, then the next thing I heard was footsteps on metal.

'I'm going upstairs.'

The spiral staircase was a distinctive feature of her apartment and she caught her breath at the top.

'You probably don't have much time to read at the moment.'

'I manage a few pages before I go to sleep. I'm reading an enthralling book at the moment about a cruise liner's journey from India to England in the 50s.'

There was a squeak of leather.

'Well, this find in the loft has whetted your nautical appetite.'

'It came recommended, in The Times I think.'

'Really?'

My mother stopped reading the papers years ago and put the weekly money in a savings account for Hope.

'How things have changed. Back in the 1950s and 60s the crew pandered completely to the whims and eccentricities of the privileged few. Did you know that many First Class passengers were actually permitted to travel with their pets and livestock was often transported in the hold?'

Was I trying to be too clever with my tactics?

'Well it sounds a far cry from the kitsch of the 1970s. I'm sure by the time we travelled with P&O, health and hygiene were probably on their case.'

I laughed.

'I think you're right, I don't remember seeing anyone travelling with their dog.'

'Did you know the Captain's name was Peter Love? He had a parrot.'

'You're fooling around.'

'Not at all. I couldn't resist a man in a smart uniform.'

I looked down.

'Hang on a sec…'

The puppy training had a little way to go and I threw Amber some kitchen roll.

'Amber, could you?'

My mother whistled a happy tune through her teeth and I could picture her smiling.

'Listen, I think a dog was an excellent idea, especially for Hope. It seemed very hard on her when Bonny went.'

I sighed.

'I know. Lottie was just the tonic we needed.'

I heard Keith's voice in the background.

'Oh yes, I'd forgotten, I'm going to a wine tasting at the rowing club this evening and I'm in a bit of a rush.'

I backtracked.

'How did you know the Captain had a parrot?'

'Let's say it's my secret and leave it at that.'

Even by my mother's standards, the story about the parrot sounded a little far-fetched.

'And what does Amber think about raking up all this stuff from your past?'

I knew by her more serious tone she was worried that I might be looking for answers where none were to be found. I looked across at Amber, who was scrutinising the menu card with a magnifying glass and scribbling notes on a pad.

'If I'm honest, she finds the whole story fascinating and she would make an excellent detective, all she needs is a pipe and a deerstalker.'

Amber pretended to puff provocatively on an imaginary pipe. I pinched her side playfully and she gestured rudely with two fingers.

'Sherlock Holmes is alive and kicking in my kitchen.'

The clock was running down and I felt I had one last chance to pin her down.

'Before you go, do you think there is a possibility that any of your friends from the cruise lived up here?'

I knew my mother thought this White House business, as she called it, was just a set of incredible coincidences.

'Why is it so important? It was 30 years ago,' she replied.

I felt she was being evasive.

'It just is,' I said, as matter-of-factly as I could muster.

Her voice softened. She clearly didn't want an argument or any more interrogation.

'I'm not being very helpful. Why don't you ask your father?'

My father, great. If there was anything more to tell, she wasn't letting on. It was another dead end.

'I might just do that when he returns from watching the cricket in South Africa.'

Amber nudged me.

'Oh, one last thing, did you find any more photographs?'

'No luck I'm afraid. And what about this ghastly business in the Lake District? Goodness, it brought back all sorts of terrible memories. Are you sure you're OK?'

I had completely forgotten I had told her and I crossed the room to the French doors, out of earshot. Outside, the brooding shadows of the distant hills were an unsettling presence and for a heartbeat my resolve wavered: perhaps I should tell my mother about the recurring nightmares too.

I kept my voice at a murmur.

'We certainly won't be going back.'

'I'm not surprised. Look, it's Hope's birthday on the 21st, what would she like? I hear it's all horses and ponies at the moment.'

'She would love more riding lessons.'

'I'll send a cheque. Amber hovered at my shoulder and gesticulated with her hand.

'Hold on, before you go…'

She scribbled two words on a piece of paper: TELL HER.

A few minutes later, Amber found me staring out of the window and wrapped her arms round my waist.

'Well…?'

I saw her reflection in the glass.

'She thinks I'm suffering from post-traumatic shock and I should consider more counselling. Bloody counselling, they must make a fortune out of people like me.'

A muscle in my jaw pulsed, a sure sign that something was still eating away inside me. I broke free and moved to a small sofa opposite the Aga, where the remnants of my past lay on a small coffee table. I turned to Amber.

'This house in the next village. It's just a house, made of bricks and mortar, and this girl I dreamt about, she's just…'

Amber shrugged.

'My mother always said you never forget your first love.'

I threw my arms in the air.

'OK, let's leave it at that.'

I scooped up the photographs from the table and put them back in the envelope.

'It's a lot of fuss about nothing. I'm clearly a middle-aged man fighting his demons. End of.'

9

The following day the post actually arrived before midday and a solitary envelope with a local postmark lay on the mat. I picked it up and opened it, scanning the letter for meaningful words. I read it again. The owners of our house had returned unexpectedly from America and had given me two months' notice.

I slumped in an armchair, my scarf still wound round my neck. I balled my fists. This was not happening.

We had settled into our new life, Hope was happy and making friends at the local primary school and for the first time since Anna's death, a certain peace had replaced the excruciating sadness. I flung the letter into the waste bin. How was I going to break the news to Hope? I couldn't bear the thought of letting her down again. I grabbed my phone from the kitchen and punched a familiar number into the keypad.

Come on, pick up…

When Amber answered she sounded distracted.

'I was just finishing off some work.'

'Sorry to call, I'm just...'

I paused.

'Is everything OK? You sound down in the dumps.'

'I've been given two months' notice by the landlord.'

'Why?'

I read the crumpled letter to her.

Her voice returned to being upbeat.

'What can I do to help?'

I sighed.

'Have you got a magic wand?'

'You could come here for a while.'

'You don't have enough room.'

'Look, I'll come round tomorrow. We'll brainstorm this thing over coffee. Two months is plenty of time to find somewhere. I'll start asking around right away.'

'Thanks, you're a saint.'

'Chin up. We'll speak tomorrow. Go and get some fresh air, clear your head.'

She was about to end the call.

'Wait. I keep thinking this is all…'

'Stop right there. No more negative thoughts. You can't keep blaming yourself. Oh and don't say anything to Hope.'

'OK, see you tomorrow.'

I put the phone down and felt the pull of addiction tugging at me. I decided a long walk would help and went upstairs to change into something more suitable. In the bedroom I changed my mind and decided to put on my running kit. I flushed the toilet which groaned like an old man with indigestion.

'Ghosts,' I whispered.

No more threatening than the pipes in this old house.

In the garage I became distracted and rummaged in the freezer for the remnants of a cottage pie when my mobile emitted the familiar bars of a blues song.

Amber shrieked down the phone.

'Where have you been?'

I noticed I had 2 missed calls.

'Calm down, I was getting changed.'

Amber was in full sales mode and her words rattled out like a machine gun.

'Sorry. Look, I've been speaking to Claire whose family have lived round here for ages and only the other day she heard about a vacant barn conversion in the next village. The local farmer is desperate to get it rented out, I believe it's unfurnished, which would suit you down to the ground.'

'And breathe…'

'I am breathing, I just want to help and…'

When life took a turn for the worst, it amazed me how quickly the coping mechanism in your brain grasped the urgency of the situation. It had been most obvious after the news of Anna's car crash.

'I should go and see it. Do you know the address?'

'It's near the old mill, just follow the canal. You can't miss it, hang on…Oh this is original, it's called The New Barn. It's part of Middlewood Farm. Should be easy to find.'

'I'll go and have a look now. Is it on with anybody yet?'

'I'm not sure.'

I slapped my thigh.

'Amber, you're my saviour, I'll speak to you later.'

'Wait until you've seen it before you thank me. Now go, get your skates on.'

I had started running recently as a means of keeping fit and also to keep my depression at bay. The local fells were a runners' paradise and as I left the village I strode out past lush green fields framed by steep hills. At the brow of the hill I turned onto a stony lane that led through the woods before it weaved past a small church and descended into the next village. My body fell into a steady rhythm and as my mood lightened I started to view my predicament in a different light; I felt invigorated and the conspiracy theories slowly dissolved amidst my exertions.

I ran under a towering viaduct carrying the canal one hundred feet above me before I turned sharply onto a muddy track, towards Clarence Mill. I ran along the towpath and left the canal at the next bridge.

Once up on the single-track road I slowed to a walk and got my bearings. I looked to my right and there behind a line of small conifers was the stone arch of Middlewood Farm. A sheepdog barked and ran out of the gate. I gave it a wide berth, avoiding its unwanted attentions, eventually stopping twenty yards further on. I glanced at my watch: 20 minutes had passed since I left home.

Not bad, I thought.

I caught my breath and took in my surroundings. Through a gap in the trees, half hidden by small outbuildings, was the barn. However, it wasn't the grey stone and vaulted timber roof of the barn that caught my eye, it was the house 50 yards further along the lane. I am a rational human being and I believe in degrees of probability and chance, but this was too much of a coincidence. I leant against the wall, slowing my heart rate.

I looked away and back several times, as if I expected the White House to disappear like a mirage in the desert. Surely if Amber had known how close this property was to the farm she would have told me? I looked down the lane. I had driven from the opposite direction when I came here with Hope, which I suppose explained my confusion.

After a minute or two I turned my attention back to the barn. There was no sign to indicate it was to let.

What the hell.

I reached through the wooden gate and gently lifted the rusty hinge, which creaked as the heavy gate swung open. I crept forward on the balls of my feet, each crunching step announcing my presence to whoever might be in the vicinity. I took in my surroundings: the front lawn needed cutting and the blackberry bushes needed pruning, but there was plenty of space for a trampoline and swing ball and I imagined Hope's high-pitched squeals of delight as her thin legs bicycled above a trampoline. I smiled. On first inspection it would make a great home.

After a glance over my shoulder I walked up the steps to the front door. I must have looked a little conspicuous in my running shorts and vest, but undeterred, I continued my visual inspection of the building. The living room was spacious, with a large inglenook, brick fireplace and through French doors the kitchen-cum-diner had traditional pine cupboards and drawers. I stood stock still. Out of the corner of my eye a sixth sense alerted me to a blur of movement and I turned slowly to observe the farm buildings beyond a nettle-infested paddock.

A mild panic rose in my throat. I was trespassing and started to prepare an explanation for my presence. I listened and waited. No-one came. A plane streaked across the heavens, its vapour trail a white smudge in an indigo sky and a dog's bark caught in the wind. I laughed nervously, trotted down the steps back to the front gate and let myself out.

Across the paddock, a red tractor stood idle in a field and the cobbled courtyard of the farm was deathly quiet. Where were the sheep, the lowing cattle, the daily clatter of machinery and generators? It felt odd and after my initial excitement, negative thoughts spiralled. Was it too close to the farm? Would the owners be forever watching our every move? I needed to ask the agents for a proper viewing and meet the owners of the farm before I made any rash decisions.

I was about to move away when I felt my eyes drawn to the White House next door. The curtains were drawn, yet it stood out as a beacon amongst the drab properties in the area; a doorway to the spirit of an old ship and a girl who was never far from my thoughts. I gazed at the gabled porch and mullioned windows, the façade a face with a mouth, nose and eyes, and the questions started again. One year ago, I'd never set foot in the Peak District, never heard of this house. Now, however ridiculous it sounded, I might be living next door. Who lived here all those years ago...?

10

I ran quickly back the way I came, through the village towards home. The air was still and unusually humid as I took the fork in the road to the reservoir. By the time I reached Amber's house my arms and legs glistened with sweat.

I knocked and I rested my weight against the porch. I heard Monty bark and scrabble towards the front door.

Amber opened the door in a paint splattered old shirt and denim shorts. The dog peered between her legs.

'What a nice surprise!'

'I would have rung, but I left my mobile at home.'

I paused and caught my breath.

'I won't stay long. I just need to talk to you for a minute.'

She kissed my cheek and nudged Monty back inside. Her nose and forehead were spotted with paint.

'I'm painting an old table I bought at an auction. Come in and I'll get you a glass of water.'

I drank greedily, emptying the glass before starting on another. I wiped my mouth with the back of my hand. The dog sniffed my crotch and ran back into the garden.

'Can I ask you something?'

She looked puzzled.

'Of course.'

'Have you been to Sugar Lane?'

She frowned.

'No.'

I took a deep breath.

'The barn is next door to the White House.'

'Oh my God! Cross my heart, I had no idea. Anyway, it was Claire, you know Book Club Claire, who told me about it. I never mentioned any of this weird cruise stuff to her.'

I rested my hands on my thighs.

'OK, I believe you.'

Her features softened.

'Are you OK? Come and sit down.'

We walked through a narrow kitchen to a small conservatory where Amber was painting.

'Sit here, I'll get you more water.'

I perched on the edge of a small sofa. Through the window I could see Monty was dragging an old towel round the garden.

'Perhaps you can use all your powers of logic and try and explain what's going on here, because frankly I'm struggling.'

She laughed weakly.

'No pressure then?'

I exhaled.

'No pressure.'

Amber sat on a window seat, her face pensive for a moment while she gathered her thoughts.

'Look, normally I'm quite sceptical about all this stuff, but maybe there's…you know, a reason.'

My brow furrowed.

'A reason? I don't understand.'

'I don't know, it's difficult to put into words. Maybe there are strange forces at work.'

'Strange forces? Please stop the mumbo jumbo, next you'll be telling me that I'll be reacquainted with a girl I haven't seen for thirty years.'

'That's if she's still alive of course.'

My face hardened.

'Can we stay off the subject of ghosts?'

'Sorry, I wasn't thinking.'

We shared an uncomfortable silence.

She sat next to me and held my hand.

'Tell me about the barn. What did you think?'

I leant forward and stretched my hamstrings.

'It ticked all the boxes. It's a shame, but I think it's too big for just the two of us.'

She held up her hand.

'Stop thinking negatively. Hope will love it, especially with the farm nearby and in the spring, there'll be newborn lambs and of course **there are the horses and...**'

I cupped my chin in my hands.

'And what if they turn out to be the neighbours from hell?'

She crossed her arms defensively.

'Spit it out.'

'I just don't know if I'm happy about being beholden to landlords who live right across the garden fence. Look at where we live now. I like my space and privacy.'

'How much space and privacy do you want? Are you a closet nude sunbather?'

'Very funny.'

'Look, it's empty and it sounds like a great house. I've heard there's a games room upstairs with a dartboard and pool table. We'll be round all the time.'

'I didn't know you played darts or pool?'

She picked up her paintbrush and resumed painting the table.

'There's a lot you don't know about me...'

'The mind boggles.'

She raised her eyebrows, and pretended to play a table tennis shot with her paint brush.

I slapped her playfully on the rear.

'Enough. I'll tell you what, I'll contact the agents and go and have a proper viewing. By the way, what are you doing on Saturday?'

Amber pretended to be disinterested and opened a can of paint with a screwdriver.

'Do you want to take me out?'

'Only if you're not busy.'

She gazed absently into space.

'Let me check my diary first. I have a busy social life what with Book Club, yoga and my Friday Rose Club.'

A moment later she turned and flashed a perfect Macleans toothpaste smile.

'Of course I'm free, where are we going?'

'I'll surprise you.'

'Hmm, can't wait! By the way, do you want me to come with you when you go back to the barn? I could give you the unrivalled benefit of a woman's eye.'

'No, I should be a mature adult and go on my own.'

I felt the onset of a slight cramp and feverishly rubbed my right calf.

'By the way, it's a bitch coming up these hills.'

She looked up.

'Do you want a lift home?'

'No, you carry on with your painting, I'll take it easy.'

I glanced at my watch.

'God, look at the time, it's picking up time in an hour, I've got to get going. Are you getting Robyn?'

'No, mum is.'

I flexed my leg and wished that I had a support network like Amber's.

'Right, I'm off.'

She grabbed my hand and her voice softened.

'Listen, if it's meant to be, it's meant to be. Trust me, whatever happened in the past, happened a long time ago. It doesn't matter anymore.'

She walked me to the front door.

'I'll schedule my next viewing for tomorrow afternoon after school has finished,' I shouted from the road.

I was still in my running kit when I collected Hope and I'm sure I overheard a few mums politely discuss my toned legs. The fitness bug had infected my system and my body was getting fitter and stronger by the day.

When we arrived at the house I told Hope to wait in the car and walked up the drive past a red pickup where two men were whitewashing an external wall. The man nearest to me had a craggy weather-beaten face and a beanie hat pulled tight over his ears.

A hat, in Summer!

The other man was younger, thickset, with dark hair that framed a ruddy complexion. They worked methodically, dipping their brushes at regular intervals into a large paint container.

I coughed nervously.

'Hi. I'm here to look at the property.'

The two men turned in my direction. The older man looked me up and down. He spoke with a thick northern accent that I struggled to understand.

'I've come to see the house,' I said to the younger man.

He put his brush down and pumped my hand energetically. I winced; the greeting felt more like a test of strength.

'My name is Steven, with a V.'

Steven with a V loosened his grip.

'We were expecting you a little earlier, it's nearly lunchtime.'

The old man looked at his battered Timex watch and nodded in agreement. It appeared lunchtime was not something to interrupt. Steven stared at my attire.

'You a runner?'

His forthright tone caught me off guard.

'No, not really,' I replied.

'Smart kit 'n all.'

I tapped my stomach and forced a smile.

'I'm not a professional.'

'You should try the fells. There's always races on round here, hardy guys with the stamina of whippets.'

Steven raised his arm past the fields teeming with lambs towards the hills in the distance. I looked up to where he had pointed and pulled my running top somewhat self-consciously over my midriff.

'Once a year, the best runners in the village race up there. They race up at old Moss's. You get a cup 'n all.'

I was quite relieved when the two men turned and dropped their brushes in a bucket of water, our conversation evidently over. I cast an eye round the farm. Today it was bustling; there were large hay bales being wrapped in black tarpaulin, threshers and tractors, and a constant thrum of generators from a shed full of cows. I held my nose as a tractor sped past spreading god knows what onto the ground. The ensuing stench caught in my throat, my eyes watered and I moved hastily back towards the relative safety of the barn. As I approached the red pickup for the second time, I noticed a large shape lying in the back. Steven tapped me on the shoulder and made me jump.

'Crows peck the sheep's eyes out if they can't get up. 'Appens now and then. Lose more if winter's bad.'

I looked away.

'I guess it's nature's way.'

I looked at the men's weather-beaten faces. This way of life was different from anything else I'd known, a tough way to earn a living, especially after the plight of mad cow disease. Steven turned to the old man.

'You go for lunch. I'll let him in.'

He pulled a key from his tatty jeans and escorted me to the front door. We stood toe to toe on the front step. He was a couple of inches taller than me and needed to visit a dentist.

'We'll be back in half an hour.'

I turned and beckoned Hope to join me.

'What shall I do when I'm finished?' I shouted.

However, my voice, like our opening exchanges, was lost in the cacophony of noise.

11

Hope appeared on the landing and peered down at me.

'I love it here!'

I looked up at her through shafts of sunlight and dust motes.

'Time to go.'

When I stepped out onto the flagstone terrace, the farmers had returned and were involved in a lively discussion.

The older man gesticulated with his paint brush.

'No manners.'

Hope held my hand tightly, startled by his histrionics. I cleared my throat, unsure if it was just friendly banter or a family dispute.

'Excuse me.'

'Finished 'ave you?'

It was a statement rather than a question. My daughter eyed them suspiciously.

'Yes, thank you,' I replied.

Steven wiped his hands on his overalls and waved his arm in an arc, while the old man spat a large phlegm ball onto the ground.

'Good land this…M'father been 'ere over 80 years, sheep mainly. Best lamb in Cheshire.'

The old man hoisted his trousers up and puffed out his chest. I wanted to say something about the harsh economic climate and how I respected their work ethic, but no words came and I stood like a mute as I handed the key back. Hope pinched my leg and brought me back to the present.

'It's a great house and I'm very interested. I'll come back to you tomorrow with a decision. If that's acceptable.'

I scribbled my mobile number on the paper.

'Here, this is the best number.'

Steven looked at my hands.

''Ave you a wife?'

The question threw me off guard and for a split second I was back at Anna's grave, dropping roses onto the casket, a flash of red amongst the sods of brown earth.

'No I don't. It's just me and my daughter.'

She placed her warm hand in mine and smiled at the farmer. Steven seemed unconvinced by my reply.

'You let us know then.'

I felt their eyes on me as we walked back to the car. Hope skipped along playfully by my side.

'Are we going to live here?'

'I need to check out a few things this evening, then we'll see.'

'Well I'm moving in, and Amber and Robyn are going to live here as well.'

Deep down of course, I realised my options were limited, although I had no desire to let my guard down with my daughter.

'Really! Does Amber know about this?'

'Robyn says...'

'Well, I'm not sure it's Robyn's decision.'

Hope turned her back, arms crossed.

'Well we are.'

I bit my tongue.

'What did you say young lady?'

Hope ran through the gate to the car.

'And, I'm going to meet your girlfriend.'

Her words were like a blow to my solar plexus. We hadn't talked about the menu card since…I couldn't remember exactly, but it wasn't recently. I looked back at the house one last time, turning over in my mind the events of the last few months. I turned the key in the ignition and as fat raindrops fell on the windscreen, I reflected on her disconcertingly frank prophecy.

Her incessant chatter didn't allow me to linger on the subject. Already at this tender age her heart was set on becoming a vet and she was understandably excited by the thought of living next to Middlewood Farm.

'Tell me about the farm you stayed on when you were young.'

A warm wave of nostalgia replaced my unease and I remembered a magical place where my sister and I fished in crystal clear streams with five-shilling nets. Tar Steps. The farmhouse had cold stone floors, the beds were damp whatever time of year it was and my clothes were always full of straw. Before breakfast, our favourite task was to collect all the freshly laid eggs and place them underneath one poor, unsuspecting hen. The farmer always played along and made a big song and dance about what a special hen she was.

The memories of that simple game were as clear and uplifting as the spring water that flowed under our feet and as if reading my thoughts, the rain clouds parted and a shaft of sunlight created a multi-coloured umbrella for my happy reverie. As we both stared in awe at the huge rainbow, I realised I had important decisions to make in the next 24 hours. I closed my eyes for a second and imagined my glass of opportunity half full, how the extra space and the larger garden would be a bonus in the summer months.

If only I had thought about how exposed the property was. Of course, today the elm and oak trees stood motionless, the air still, the farmers unwilling to loosen my interest in the property with tales of extreme winter storms and gales. I turned out of the drive and momentarily glanced back.

Hope screamed.

A horn blared and I narrowly missed a delivery van speeding along the lane in the opposite direction. My hands shook as I placed them back on the wheel. I thought I had seen a girl standing in the garden next door.

-

The next morning the weather turned autumnal. The day was grey and blustery and after breakfast I suggested to Hope that we take Lottie for a walk. There followed a minor protest about her wellingtons not fitting properly, before we set off down the road in our waterproofs.

We headed east, in the direction of a nearby estuary. I loved old war stories and there was a rumour an allied WWII bomber had crashed here as it returned from its mission. Over a pint in the Robin Hood, the local quarry manager explained that many years ago the M.O.D. threatened to mark the area as a war grave, to prevent bounty hunters searching for war relics. The memory of the Dambusters was apparently alive and well in these parts.

The country lanes were deserted and after the recent shower, rainwater surged along newly forged gullies. Lottie strode out in front, straining at her leash, although it wasn't long before the road steepened and our pace slowed. Halfway up the hill, a one-eyed dog appeared from a farm entrance and we hurried past to escape its unwanted attentions. The track was rutted and muddy as it wound its way to the summit.

'Come on, let's climb to the top.'

A few yards on I spotted a gap in the dry stone wall and let Lottie off the lead. Hope scooted behind her as rabbits scattered in all directions. At the top, I found Hope peering over the edge of a large hollow full of murky water. She looked disappointed.

'There's nothing here and it stinks.'

I sniffed the air.

'Yes you're right. Come on, let's go round the other side.'

We walked round the summit, without noticing a grey mist that had begun to envelope the hill, reducing our visibility to no more than a few yards. With nothing left to hold her attention, I decided it was time to head home. Lottie and I took an adjacent path, and for a moment I lost sight of her. It was at that exact moment I heard someone shout angrily.

I clambered over the next ridge to get a better view and saw a man leaning on a gate directly below me. He shouted again.

'Hey you!' and I watched my daughter edge sheepishly down the slope towards him.

'You shouldn't be up there, get down here!'

The man didn't appear to have a gun, however I wasn't taking any chances and grabbed Lottie's collar and clipped on her lead. My pace quickened. Hope was only a few yards from the farmer. The slope was slick with mud and I slid the last few yards.

'Hope, stay where you are.'

She was clearly shaken and I fought to keep my temper under control.

'Hey mate, she's just a child.'

Her eyes filled with tears and I held out my hand to my daughter.

'Stand next to me darling.'

The man's eyes bulged and he stared directly at me.

'I'll swear in front of who I fucking like. You're on my land and if your dog chases my animals, I'll shoot it.'

I knew this was no idle threat; dogs chasing livestock were fair game for any farmer with a shotgun.

Stupid mistake.

We squared up to each other, a foot apart. At such close quarters I noticed how few teeth he had and his forehead glistened with beads of sweat. He raised an arm and I clenched my fists ready to block his blow.

He didn't strike me. Instead he poked an accusing finger at my chest. Instinctively I took a step back.

'You're not the first either, I've had it up to here with ignorant townies on my land.'

I stood my ground. My southern accent had thrown him. He had no idea we lived in the village. I briefly considered using the story about the crash site as an excuse for trespassing but decided it might rile him further.

The man jabbed his finger in my direction again.

'I'll tell you something, I'm going to do something about it, you'll see. We haven't recovered from foot and mouth and that nearly ruined us all.'

He turned away from me and spat over his shoulder.

When he turned back, all the colour had drained from his face and he clutched his chest. I reached out to steady him.

'I'm really sorry. It's my fault, not my daughter's. I didn't realise it was private land.'

He pushed my hand away.

'Are you blind as well as stupid? Can't you read the signs?'

'Look I've said sorry, we didn't see...'

'Don't you have a map? There are public footpaths. It's not a fucking picnic area, this is my land.'

'I'm sorry, we don't have a map and can you stop swearing?'

'Well, if I went to London I'd buy a fucking map.'

Hope clung to my waist as he stormed off and I knelt down and comforted her with soothing words. I just hoped he hadn't gone to get a gun. I wiped her snotty nose with my handkerchief.

'Why was that man angry?'

I put my arm round her. I wasn't sure she would understand the ins and outs of countryside law, so I skirted round the subject.

'I think he was having a bad day. We all have them occasionally don't we?'

Hope wiped her nose again with her cuff.

'Like you used to do with mummy?'

My world tilted again and I berated myself for acting like such an idiot.

'Yes, much the same.'

I took Hope in my arms and felt her wet nose against my cheek. It reminded me of how limp her body felt after I explained that her mother wasn't coming back. I looked to the heavens. Sometimes I felt like a fish out of water up here, I had nothing in common with these people and their way of life. And what of my new landlords? I wasn't sure I wanted to live next to people who slaughtered animals and shot stray dogs with guns. I grabbed Hope's hand and hurried off before the farmer returned.

-

When I met Amber later, my reservations about the impending move festered on and I was still in a state of limbo when I recounted the fracas to her as we sat on the patio. I passed her a ginger beer, waiting for her to say something. Anything. She took a long swig.

'What on earth were you thinking?'

I wasn't good at taking my own medicine and I turned away from her and watched the girls playing with Lottie in the garden.

'I'm having second thoughts about this move.'

I sensed her frustration as she shook her head in disapproval.

'Stop right there. I agree his foul language was inexcusable, especially in front of Hope, but he was right to act the way he did. I remind you constantly about staying on the footpaths and not letting Lottie chase sheep. You know the rules. Only last week I heard a terrible story about two spaniels who were shot by a farmer because they were chasing his chickens. There are different rules up here and I'm not letting you use one bad tempered man as an excuse for a change of heart. If you change your mind you have very little time to find somewhere else. Look, I've done some delving for you. The family that own the farm have been around here for ages, they are well respected in the village, so don't tar them with the same brush.'

I lowered my gaze.

'Thanks for the lecture,' I said under my breath.

She shrugged.

'I'm just telling you how I feel. Oh, this is pointless. I'm going to take Robyn home and let you sleep on it.'

I stood in front of the French doors, blocking her exit. I knew I had pushed her too far.

'Wait. Don't go. I'm sorry I was so terse with you.'

She placed her hands on her hips.

'Well stop dragging your heels. You know what, I don't think this is about conflicts and farmers.'

I nodded sheepishly because it was the truth.

'Listen. I'm telling you, you'd be really stupid to miss this opportunity. What are you scared of? Is there something from your past that is so terrible? It was thirty-odd years ago and that's a ton of water under the bridge.'

I considered fighting my corner.

She raised an eyebrow.

'Well? Is there?'

I stroked the coarse stubble on my chin.

'I'm being selfish. I should be doing this for Hope.'

She pointed a finger in my direction.

'Exactly.'

'You're right. I can't let a few nightmares sabotage my life.'

'Hallelujah. Well, that seems to have put an end to all that nonsense. Now, when are you moving in?'

12

The next day I phoned the agents and after a short negotiation over deposits I agreed to rent the barn. My new landlords were Mr and Mrs Steven (with a V) Ward and the agents promised to fax over the relevant paperwork that afternoon.

Please God, let this be a happy house, I thought as I signed the agreement.

We moved in on July 11th, which by another twist of fate was also Amber's birthday. I turned the radio up as the weather forecaster confidently predicted Sunday would be the hottest day of the year so far. She explained that the unusual heatwave was courtesy of the sub-tropical jet stream which was lying much further north than in previous years.

Summer had truly arrived and we toiled hard in the sweltering heat, ferrying furniture and packing cases from the van into the house. It was back-breaking work, made all the more uncomfortable by a swarm of flying ants that drove us back into the house for about half an hour. Shortly afterwards, my one-man assembly line was halted by a water pistol fight with the children. I was grateful for Amber coming to my rescue with the hose and even though we were soaked through, at 6 o'clock the last box was hauled up the steps and deposited safely inside the house.

I left Amber and the two girls flaked out on the front lawn, while I disappeared into the kitchen to prepare a tray of iced drinks. Inside, the air was cool and I stood at the bottom of the stairs and searched for the house's soul, its heart. I listened for a response: an eave creaking, a gurgling pipe, a radiator ticking. There was nothing; the house was deathly quiet.

For weeks I had tried to imagine myself living here. I knew I should have been elated; instead I felt subdued, riddled once again with self-doubt. I moved along the hall and stared at the White House through a porthole window. Would the dreams follow me here? In the far distance, fields of yellow flax stretched as far as the eye could see and I thought about what Amber had said. Maybe there was a reason.

I stopped at the front door and put the tray down on a table in the hall. Hope looked up and smiled at me and for a brief moment I was envious of her, envious of her youth and her untainted innocence. Amber crept up behind me and brought me out of my catatonic state and I physically melted into her arms as she nuzzled my neck.

'Penny for them?'

I hadn't realised how exhausted I was and my smile was tight, a little forced.

'What's up?'

'I'm just praying I've made the right decision.'

She turned me round.

'Look at this beautiful house, you are going to be really, really happy here. Have you seen how happy Hope is?'

I wiped my brow with dusty hands.

'I know, I'll feel differently in a few days. I could sleep for a week.'

She clapped her hands.

'Right! Don't do any more unpacking this evening. It can all wait. I'm going home now and I'll bring Lottie back tomorrow.'

I mumbled a gratitude.

'Earth to Paul? Just make sure you feed Hope and get an early night.'

I took her hand in mine.

'Listen, thanks for all your help. Oh, I almost forgot.'

I bent down and retrieved a brown paper bag from the hall.

'It's not been the most relaxing birthday you've ever had, so go home and spoil yourself this evening.'

'When did you have time?'

She hugged me and I could feel her hot breath on my neck.

'Mmm you're sweaty, and you know what? I like it.'

In the small bag was a DVD of her favourite film and a large bar of Green and Black's chocolate.

She kissed me tenderly on the lips.

'Oh and I have something for your new house.'

Amber ran towards her car and reappeared with a picture in a frame.

'I did one of Robyn's entry as well.'

A burger in a bun oozed ketchup, while underneath there was a plate of colourful vegetables: "Burgers are banned, Veggies are Grand."

'I thought it was a brilliant idea. Maybe she has a future in ecology or marketing.'

We stood together on the front steps and I wanted to talk to her about my fears, but I knew she would only tell me I was being paranoid again.

Amber pinched my bottom, much to the amusement of the children.

'Be good you two, and I'll see you tomorrow.'

Hope and I ran across the lawn waving frantically like scarecrows caught in a gale and when we could no longer see the rear of the battered Audi we turned and I placed my arm protectively around my daughter.

'You must be starving.'

Hope pulled me into the hall.

'I want spaghetti.'

I clapped my hands.

'Spaghetti with meatballs and my famous tomato sauce it is.'

I was about to close the front door when a gunshot rang out across the valley and three large crows left a nearby tree in an explosion of wings and noise. Hope threw her arms round my waist as we prepared to spend our first night in yet another house.

A few days later, a small brown package arrived. I spilled the contents out onto the kitchen table. Along with a card with a picture of a large dog squeezed into a small kennel, there were two photographs. I read the accompanying note with renewed interest.

Dear Paul,

I do hope this is the end of your housing jinx and the move wasn't too stressful. Sorry I wasn't around to help, Keith's mother is very ill and we had to visit her at short notice.

I found these photographs while searching for some old family documents. You probably don't know but over the last year I've been expending a lot of time and energy trying to trace my family through Ancestry.com. My goal is to complete a detailed family tree for my side of the family, the Freathys. I'll show you sometime.

I think there were more photographs but over the passage of time they've almost all disappeared. I should have put them in an album shouldn't I? Anyway here are the infamous E deck gang in all their glory? Sadly you are not in either photograph, although that could be you, kneeling in the front. I must say it made me smile, you look such a happy bunch. and look at the clothes and hairstyles.

I hope this will bring back happy memories and, maybe you can find out if any of them lived in that house you mentioned.

Lots of love
And looking forward to my visit
Kisses and hugs to Hope
PS On the way to Norfolk I went to Anna's grave and left some flowers from you and Hope.
PPS How's Amber?
Mum xxxx

I tried to dodge the arrows of lament that were certain to pierce my heart in a matter of moments. It was impossible. My life was a Pandora's box of lies and deceit and I felt a prolonged sense of regret as I put the letter and photographs on the hall table.

I put the kettle on and calmed my troubled mind enough to allow me to study the first photograph. The quality was not great, but then what could one expect from an old Kodak Instamatic. I ran my finger over the image: four children sat on a leather sofa, the tongue and groove wood panelling strangely at odds with any ship I've ever been on. The boys had long hair, smart shirts and fat ties; one girl had a green garland round her head while the other wore a yellow dress.

All interesting enough, but my eyes were drawn to the third girl perched on the arm of the sofa. She had a symmetrical bob and was dressed in a white pinafore dress and matching boots. I caught my breath. Her face had an innocent beauty, although her eyes were an eerie red, a result of the cheap flash bulb. Was this the girl in my dream?

I looked at the second photograph. A three-piece band played on a small stage while two boys in flared trousers and tank tops stood nearby. A sixth sense made me speculate about whether one of them was Twig? I flipped the photo over, but like the first, there were no names on the back.

I returned to the first photograph, dismissing my disappointment. If this was the E deck gang, why were we all dressed in our Sunday best? My head spun and I held the Polaroid up to the light, willing a fragment of memory to return.

As I pinned the photographs on the kitchen noticeboard, I glanced at the clock above it.

3.15.

I cursed under my breath and grabbed my car keys.

As I drove up the winding lanes, I reflected on how I missed the nearness of our old house to the school. If I went for a run, which I usually did most mornings, there was never enough time in the afternoons to get everything done.

At the gate, I acknowledged a few parents I knew by name and chatted briefly with Robyn's grandmother before Hope pulled me away, nattering on about some Haflinger foals she had heard Louisa talk about. She took me on a detour to a farm at Ingersley Vale, where we were met by a fresh-faced lady in riding gear. The fresh air cleared my head and while Hope ran excitedly from stable to stable, I sat on a small stone bridge and watched a stream cascade noisily over a granite outcrop into the wishing pool below. I wished for an end to my tortured nights.

Hope still had a handful of carrots in her pockets when we arrived home and while she went upstairs to change out of her dirty school clothes and wash her hands, I began to prepare Friday night's tea. I had paid a visit to the local butchers in the morning and this evening I was baking chicken breasts with mozzarella and cherry tomatoes.

I placed the ingredients haphazardly into the ovenproof dish, although as I searched for the roll of baking foil, a nagging doubt drew me back to the noticeboard.

What if the girl had lived in the house next door?

It was unlikely, but not impossible. I remembered Amber's words from a few weeks ago and I shivered uneasily: did something happen on the cruise? The sinister thought made my skin crawl and I urged myself to be a little less fanciful: how many ghosts can one man have?

After dinner I reached for my mobile and stopped in mid-dial. This was completely the wrong time to be burdening Amber with my anxieties and she had made it patently clear she didn't want to be disturbed tonight due to work commitments. I loaded the dishwasher and joined Hope and Lottie in the lounge, where we all shared a bag of popcorn while watching the film Seabiscuit for the umpteenth time.

By the time I had read to Hope for a good half an hour, my energy reserves were exhausted and I hurriedly let Lottie out, locked up and climbed into bed. Seconds before the blanket of sleep smothered me, I was bombarded by conflicting voices.

We just need to probe a little more.

Then:

Some secrets should remain buried.

I was trapped. I ran blindly back along the corridor praying there was a way out. My heart pounded as I realised it was another dead end. The overhead lights flashed on and off and slowly the cabin doors began to open. I began to cry, heavy, snotty sobs. What did they want? I screamed for help but it was too late.

13

I was released from my dream by a faint tapping that grew steadily louder, until I could stand it no longer and was forced to leave the warmth of my bed and investigate. I instinctively grabbed a tennis racket and followed the strange tapping sound. I crept downstairs and stopped outside the study.

I pushed the door open. The room was empty and still. I walked outside and inspected the window; there was no significant damage, just bird droppings on the sill and smeared grot on the mirrored glass.

I returned to my bed as the light of a new day grazed the surrounding hills and as I slept on deep into Saturday morning, it was those same noises I subsequently replayed in my mind as I re-imagined Hitchcock's terrifying film The Birds.

Hope eventually dragged me from my bed at 11am and I trudged downstairs like a zombie to make breakfast. I finally got my act together and produced something that resembled eggy bread and we sat side by side at the breakfast bar, dipping bite-size pieces into ketchup. I was distracted from my last few mouthfuls by two ducks landing in the garden. Lottie ran to the French doors and let them know they were trespassing, although the courting couple seemed unimpressed by her high-pitched bark and waddled sedately past, not a care in the world.

While Hope put the plates in the dishwasher, I wrote a reminder to myself to ask the farmers about our other visitors, because the last thing I needed now was for Hope to be scared by noises in the night.

It was already midday when Lottie alerted us to the Royal Mail van and I threw on some trainers and dashed out hoping to catch him. He was a friendly guy and I wanted to thank him for recommending the perfect tick remover for Lottie. I reached the gate and waved but I was too late as the van disappeared in a cloud of dust. I unlocked the mailbox and there amongst the bills and junk mail was a handwritten invitation from my neighbours.

I went back inside and placed it on the mantelpiece, as one did in the days of balls and dinner parties. It had surprised me and I was unsure how to react; should I be flattered or guarded? In a quandary, I decided to deal with my feelings later and instead busied myself with a little car maintenance as my MOT was due soon. After we had taken Lottie for a walk, I retrieved the invitation and rang Amber. She answered on the second ring.

'An invitation from Middlewood Farm! Blimey, are you going to go?'

I couldn't hear her above the noise of racing cars and so I muted Wacky Races, much to Hope's annoyance.

'I suppose I ought to. I don't want to start off on the wrong foot and it would be an opportunity to meet the family. By the way, it says "plus one"...'

I hadn't been very forthcoming about my current relationship status and I had no idea how Amber would respond. She had made it perfectly clear she was happy to talk about my past with Anna but she wasn't quite ready to fill her shoes.

'Are you asking me to be your "plus one"?'

I crossed my fingers behind my back.

'I'd certainly feel more comfortable if you came.'

Amber hmmmd.

'I can't see what harm it would do.'

I pumped my fist in the air.

'I could do with a rest from all this paperwork. I'll speak to mum and sort out the kids. Is it a smart or casual affair?'

I looked at the card.

'I have no idea. Sunday best I guess.'

'I'll see you tomorrow at 12 then, kiss kiss.'

I was about to end the call when I remembered something.

'Wait, I almost forgot. Mum sent me some photographs.'

'Of the cruise?'

'Yes, and guess what, there's one of the E deck gang.'

'And...?'

I kept my voice to a whisper in case Hope was listening.

'It's her.'

'Wow, are you sure?'

'100 percent.'

'Jesus. If what you're saying is true. What if...'

'I know, I've been thinking of nothing else since,' I snapped.

I didn't want to mention the birds at the window; my sanity was on the line here.

'OK, calm down, I'm only trying to help.'

I took a deep breath.

'I'm sorry, it's just that I had another nightmare last night.'

'Look, you can't continue like this. You'll make yourself ill.'

I rubbed my eyes and continued with my minor deception.

'I hoped the dreams would stop after we moved here. It's like this girl is following me.'

I heard papers rustling.

'Shit. Look, I need to call a client in America, let's talk about this tomorrow. I think it's time we started asking your new neighbours some questions.'

The more I thought about the impending lunch, the more apprehensive I became. My recent meetings with local farmers had hardly been harmonious and the altercation from a few weeks ago had left a bitter taste in my mouth.

-

I pulled a few hangers from the wardrobe and threw them on the bed. Amber was in the bathroom fussing over her hair and I had to shout to make myself heard over Hope's hairdryer.

'If it turns out to be the afternoon from hell, we can always use the children as an excuse for leaving early.'

She appeared wearing white linen trousers and matching vest.

'What do you think?'

Her casual school gate chic had been replaced by something more elegant and stylish. Understated but sexy, and all I could do was stand and stare.

She put her hands on her hips.

'Say something then…'

I whistled before adding, 'Bellissimo,' although I was more than a little distracted as I tried to decide which pair of loafers to wear. She looked me up and down. I wore shorts and a white shirt. My favorite Aviator sunglasses were propped up on my head.

'Very cool. You look like you should be on a film set. Do you think we're a little overdressed?

I took a step towards her.

'Well we'll soon find out. Come here, you look good enough to eat.'

She held me at arm's length.

'It's hot enough without you raising the temperature further.'

I skulked off and retrieved my watch from the bathroom.

'And let's not forget the menu card and the photographs, it'll make a nice ice-breaker.'

I frowned.

'They'll take one look at me and think I'm having a midlife crisis.'

She held out a hand.

'Give them to me,' and she placed them in her bag.

In the hall, I was mesmerised by the movement of her bottom as it wiggled towards the front door. I couldn't help myself and surreptitiously slid my arm round her waist as she made one last check in the full-length mirror.

She wriggled free, her tone sterner.

'We have to go and I don't want my hair or make up messed up, OK?'

I acquiesced.

'Maybe later?'

I caught a hint of a sparkle in her eyes as she checked herself one last time in the mirror by the door.

'Maybe.'

I opened the door.

'And while we're on the subject of the White House, who said that a family lived there all those years ago?'

She lifted a finger in the air.

'I did.'

'Listen Miss Marple, you don't know that. It's just a hunch.'

She tapped her nose with an index finger.

'I know it is, but my hunches are usually correct. Come on, let's go and mingle with your neighbours.'

The doors from a small barn were flung open and music filled the courtyard. I nudged Amber's arm.

'"Stuck in the Middle with You", remember the scene in Reservoir Dogs?'

I was currently the undisputed champion when we played beat the intro in the car.

She slapped her thigh.

'I knew it, I'm just too slow on the buzzer.'

She grasped my arm and pointed through a gap in the small conifers.

'Look, there's a few more people here than you imagined.'

She stopped in mid-stride.

'Have you got the wine?'

I smacked a hand against my forehead.

'Shit, I forgot!'

It was too late to turn back. We'd been spotted. Carol put a tray of meat down and waved. Even from this distance she looked remarkably like her brother Steven. She left the barbeque unattended for a moment and walked over to open the gate, followed by two Jack Russells.

Small groups of people stood around the cobbled courtyard and I felt like we'd boarded our very own time machine as Tony Christie crooned "Show Me the Way to Amarillo". Pungent aromas of smoked hickory wafted into the air as we watched Carol's husband stack the grill with a variety of prime cuts, while in the shade of a sycamore tree, their father, his face the colour of a pickled walnut, puffed away on his pipe.

Carol's husband wiped his hands on his apron and shook my hand.

'Glad you could make it. I'm Peter, now who's this lovely lady?'

'This is Amber my…'

Steven spared me any further interrogation.

'What'd you like to drink Amber?'

'Glass of wine would be great.'

'Wine you say?'

Peter immediately disappeared at speed into the house. Amber blushed and shuffled from one foot to another. I noticed a nearby table was already littered with cider bottles and cans of beer, but not a bottle of wine in sight. It appeared we had already caused a stir.

'Maybe he's sneaked out to buy some,' I whispered.

Amber placed a finger on my lips.

'Shhh.'

An uncomfortable interlude passed before Peter reappeared, cradling a bottle in his arms. He looked at the label and proffered it to Amber. He was out of breath.

'Jacob's Creek. It's red.'

I thought considering the weather a chilled rosé might have been a better choice, but I kept my thoughts to myself. Peter poured a generous amount into a glass.

'Try some.'

Amber took a small sip and smiled gratefully.

'Delicious, thank you.'

One could sense his relief and he swiftly refilled Amber's glass to the brim.

A man with a pot belly and a lady in riding gear sidled over and glasses were raised.

'To our new neighbours, may their stay be a long and happy one. Cheers everyone.'

I brushed my lips against Amber's ear.

'Have you seen the film Deliverance?'

Amber kicked my shin as Steven handed me a can of local bitter. Within minutes I had broken golden rule number one.

'Come and meet my wife.'

She had large breasts and rosy cheeks, and spoke in a broad northern dialect which I struggled to understand. I exchanged glances with Amber and smiled politely; it seemed the most agreeable response. I still felt like a fish out of water and even though I hadn't mentioned it to Amber, I planned a hasty exit after the meal.

After the introductions, a frail lady in a pale blue dress placed cutlery and glasses on a large oak table and we took our places for lunch. I sat next to Steven while Amber found herself sandwiched between Carol and Steven's wife, Elaine. Steven seemed amiable enough after a few drinks and chatted candidly about rural life, and how his family had farmed the land between the canal and the Kerridge ridge for three generations. They had been, along with their cousins who ran the butcher's shop, an integral part of village life for over 100 years.

The beer was hoppy and strong and I felt the satisfying rush of my old enemy as it flowed through my veins, and my initial concerns were quashed as no-one seemed the least bit interested in my marital status or what I did for a job. We even cleared up the little matter of our nighttime visitors, with a warning from Steven about a murder of large crows that frequented the nearby woods. The afternoon was disappearing fast and it seemed like a good time to broach the subject of the White House. I was about to ask Amber for the menu card when Steven excused himself and his elderly father edged onto the bench next to me.

He was in his eighties and hard of hearing and for the moment I didn't feel comfortable prying any further. Instead, I let him ramble on about his farm and his sheep. He pointed out the buildings that had been recently renovated and how three generations of the same family now lived communally round a central courtyard. I couldn't think of anything more claustrophobic and steered the conversation onto the history of our new house. It had been built on reclaimed land and finished about 10 years ago. I sensed he was immensely proud of the property he had built with his son.

'Hard as nails' was a phrase that sprang to mind.

He was still as strong as an ox and I had seen him sheep shearing and riding in the pick-up with his dogs on daily head counts. As the afternoon wore on, I got a definite sense of a man who had toughed life out even when his health had been a concern.

Our conversation was a little one way, but I listened patiently as he showed me how to fill his favourite pipe with tobacco. He moved the match carefully over the pipe bowl and the flame gently caressed the tobacco. He inhaled rhythmically before snuffing the match out with jaundiced fingers.

The old man proceeded to have a coughing fit and as his family fussed over him, I looked around at the buildings and the vehicles and decided to revise my earlier land rich, cash poor evaluation. A hard slap on my shoulder brought me out of my reverie.

He caught his breath.

'You've brought good weather with you, now be a good lad and help me up.'

I watched him shuffle over to his wife sitting in the shade under the sycamore tree. He was, I reflected, a man of old-fashioned virtues, although something told me he wasn't willing to hand over control of his farm yet.

Afternoon drifted into evening. The faltering sun dipped lower in the sky and as if by magic, like fairy lights at Christmas time, pin pricks of light illuminated the outbuildings. Music boomed from the barn again and I stood at the entrance, like a teenager at a school disco. Out of the blue, Carol pulled me onto the dancefloor and I self-consciously looked around for Amber.

'Come on, shake a leg.'

The 1960s music swirled and rose, building to a crescendo, as sweaty bodies threw their arms **in** the air and sang along to the vocals. I did my best to feel uninhibited and after the first song my limbs loosened and I found myself enjoying the sheer madness of it all. After a few dances I stepped outside to catch my breath and replenish my glass with water. I leant against the wall and observed the cavorting, shouting and drinking. The partying was earthy and primitive, edgy, and like nothing I had witnessed before. It had not though changed my opinion: I had nothing in common with these people.

It was then I heard shrieks of laughter coming from the room upstairs. I stumbled up a narrow staircase and as I reached the top, I found Amber. She was playing darts with Peter's cousins.

'120. Your go, Jeremy. I'm going to sit the next round out because I've just seen my fancy man.'

Now an ex-con who used to work with me on shoots told me if you ever come up against anyone who is seriously good at table tennis or darts, they've either been brought up in a pub or probably spent some time at Her Majesty's pleasure. Which, in my inebriated state, left me musing about Amber's formative years.

She weaved her way in my direction and pulled me down onto a threadbare sofa, her roving hands exploring my chest. She turned my head with her hand and with the skill of a hypnotist her piercing blue eyes cast their spell.

We were just about to kiss passionately when Amber apparently had a change of heart and removed her hand from under my shirt.

'I'm just going to phone mum and make sure the kids are in bed. I left my mobile outside, so stay here, I'll be back before you know I've gone.'

I self-consciously fiddled with the buttons on my shirt.

'You're drunk as a skunk.'

She pressed a finger to my lips.

'Sshhh. I'm having a ball and they're such lovely people… I'll be back in a minute,' and with that she slipped comically off the sofa onto the floor before disappearing like a slalom skier down the stairs.

Five minutes became ten and I returned to the courtyard to find a line of drunken revellers dancing the conga. Peter appeared as if from nowhere and like Baloo in "The Jungle Book", led the winding column round the yard. My jaw dropped as they passed me again: Amber had joined the line and Peter clung onto her shapely behind. She looked drunkenly amused as she hopped past and fearing the worst I grabbed her arm, extricating her from Peter's licentious clutches.

The conga soon ran out of steam and very soon the sky to the west was transformed from dark blue into a myriad of violet, orange and rich crimson. When the glowing orb finally sank below the horizon, the final smudges of colour in the sky were replaced by a dark brooding nightscape. It was a fitting end to a remarkable day and also the signal for guests to start drifting home, in our case a hilarious drunken meander through the paddock. It was now occupied by four large tups which Amber ran away from because she thought they were albino cows.

-

I was jolted awake, by an orchestra of tiny hammers chipping away at my skull. I felt guilt-ridden: I would have to take my vow of abstinence all over again. I was unsure whose bedroom I was in until I felt Lottie jump on the bed.

'I'm hanging up my drinking boots,' I said to the dog, who nudged her way under my arm. I rubbed her tummy tenderly and she responded by placing her head in my lap. Maybe Amber was right all along, it was going to be different living on the farm, but that didn't mean it couldn't be fun and invigorating. The curtains were still drawn and I explored the other side of the bed with my other hand. It was empty.

I eased my body gingerly out of bed and padded downstairs to the kitchen to make breakfast. Ten minutes later the smell of freshly brewed coffee and grilled bacon lured Amber downstairs. She appeared a little unsteadily at the kitchen door in a night shirt that was indecently short. Even allowing for the hangover from hell, my eyes spent a little too long on her slender legs.

'How did you sleep? I can't even remember how we got home.'

She tugged at the nightshirt in the forlorn hope that a few more inches of material would cover her bum.

'Terribly. Your snoring is loud enough to wake the dead. I tried everything, not even a sharp knee in the back would stop you. At one point I contemplated smothering you with a pillow and eventually took myself off to the spare room for some peace and quiet.'

'Sorry. Double whammy then. You get a bad night's sleep and I've mislaid the menu card and photographs.'

She yawned.

'Oh shit, we forgot didn't we? Hang on a moment.'

Amber rummaged through her handbag hanging on a coat hook by the back door.

'It's OK, they're safe.'

I poured coffee.

'I'll just have to wait for another opportunity, and let's be honest, a few days here or there isn't going to make any difference.'

She rubbed her temples.

'That house has a lot to answer for.'

I turned the bacon.

'You know, apart from the gardener, I still haven't seen any sign of life next door.'

She looked absently out of the kitchen window.

'How does he do it? His legs must be hollow. I'm not drinking for a week.'

I turned my head. Peter was in the courtyard, his white rugby shirt emblazoned with the Cross of St George.

'He's been up for ages, and I know what you're thinking, but no, not Peter. Not this morning.'

'OK, let's leave it for today. By the way, have you any painkillers because my head is banging.'

Amber took her coffee and bacon roll and curled up in the snug. She placed her mug on the window ledge and stretched her arms and legs in such a sensual way that I found my arousal button pushed and there was nothing I could do about it.

My voice dropped to a husky whisper.

'The girls won't be back for a while.'

Amber rolled her eyes, but it was too late. In one easy movement I lifted her off the sofa and carried her towards the stairs. Amber squeezed my bicep as I back-heeled the bedroom door shut.

'My what strong arms you have Benjamin Bear.'

-

I often wondered if I had done or said something contentious that evening, because no further invitations were to grace my doormat for quite some time.

The following morning we got our first break: I dropped Hope at school and with my resolve hardened, I walked down the lane to the White House with a letter meant for them. The house of secrets, I thought to myself as I stood in front of the detached white bricked villa: a silent sentinel that maintained a vigil over its immaculate gardens.

At that precise moment a black cat jumped down from an ivy-covered wall and crossed my path. I am not overly superstitious, although I have always been deeply suspicious of cats, an aversion that runs, long and deep. My first memory was my grandmother's large white cat Sheba, the same grandparents who lived near the cemetery. The cat was friendly enough, except for the decapitated trophies she brought into the kitchen and the severe allergic reactions I suffered, which inevitably meant we had to pack up and leave for home before my conditioned worsened.

I tried to stay away from cats, which I did successfully until I was invited to a sleepover at a Prep school friend's house. We stayed up until midnight watching a black and white horror film entitled The Black Cat. I never a slept a wink that night or for weeks afterwards and even today I can't bear to be in the same room as one.

I waved my arms.

'Shoo. Go and find your mate.'

The cat stood its ground.

'Shoo!'

It slinked forward and wound its body round my legs, purring contentedly. It set my teeth on edge in much the same way that nails on a blackboard do and I nudged it firmly with my foot. The cat sensed I was someone not to mess with and it skulked off into the undergrowth.

The house watched me approach. It felt like I was stepping back into the past as I nervously trudged up the steps to the porch. I pulled back the ornate brass knocker.

From inside a phone rang. I jumped backwards, my heart raced. It continued to ring.

No answering machine.

I held my breath and counted to ten and then I changed my mind; for better or worse I posted the letter through the letterbox and headed home. The house was not going to give up its secrets easily.

I stood in the garden, looked out across the divide and listened to sheep bleating in the surrounding fields. It was an idyllic midsummer day and the trees and shrubs that lined the border between our properties were in full bloom. If I stood on tiptoe I could just see the top of a large conservatory that extended across the back of their house. I wondered if this impressive barrier of flora would be such an effective barrier in winter. My thoughts were interrupted by an unexpected knock at the front door.

A geriatric man stood on the step and offered his hand in greeting.

'We live next door, my…'

I smiled knowingly.

'Mr Royle.'

His voice was hoarse.

'Yes, that's right.'

He pressed a handkerchief to his rather bulbous nose and blew it noisily. A woman who I presumed was his wife appeared as if by magic by his side and started to speak, stuttered, then stopped. I waited patiently for the frail woman to continue.

'One of our caaaaaa cats is missssss…ing.'

Mr Royle gestured with his hand and she held up a laminated card with a picture of a black cat and a phone number.

'Can you check your garage and shed. She mmmm may be hiding ssssss somewhere.'

Her stutter was dreadful and I waited a few moments to make sure she had finished.

'Lottie usually lets us know if they're around.'

I smiled politely and tried to look like a concerned neighbour. I didn't tell them I encouraged the dog to chase the cats when they came into our garden.

'I will get Hope to have a good look around. I'm sure she'll turn up.'

'Thank you Paul, it is Paul isn't it? So nice to meet you eventually.'

'Yes, likewise, I was beginning to think the house was empty.'

Mr Royle placed the handkerchief over his nose again and took a step forward.

'We're retired now, off seeing the world if we're not down with the bloody flu.'

His wife held on to his arm.

'Although on our last Med cruise, half the guests haaaaad foooood…'

A cruise.

I felt nervous laughter building in my stomach. Mr Royle finished her sentence for his wife.

'Poisoning, and I've been writing letters of complaint for weeks, but still not a penny in compensation.'

I shrugged.

'That's big companies for you.'

'Come on Lyn, let's leave this young man in peace, I'm sure he doesn't want to hear our…'

Actually I did.

There followed an uncomfortable silence during which I started an imaginary conversation with the old couple.

Before you go Mr Royle could I ask you a few questions. It won't take a minute. It's just that I am conducting an investigation into some local properties.

At that point I would laugh uneasily.

No, I'm not an historian. You see Mr Royle, I found this menu card. It was from a cruise I went on in 1974. I was only thirteen. While we were on board a group of rag-tag children formed a gang. It was called the E deck gang. One particular girl in the gang became a special friend of mine and I believe there's a remote possibility she may have lived in your house. No, I'm not a raving lunatic, I have photographs to prove it. And look, here's your address right here.

Mrs Royle studied me with renewed interest, before she took her husband's arm and hurried him away towards the gate. I followed them down the steps,

'Wait. Can I ask you a question?'

Mr Royle turned, as a gust of wind swept strands of white hair across his forehead.

'Of course you can.'

'How long have you lived here?'

He seemed puzzled by my question and looked to his wife for assistance.

'Now let me think. The memory is not as good as it used to be.'

I leant against the gate, a small tremor of excitement building in the pit of my stomach.

'We moved here in the mid-80s, so around twenty years.'

And then he sneezed three times in a row. I tried to keep my composure.

'Did you know the previous owners?'

I understood why a question like this might seem a little odd to someone I'd only met a few minutes ago. He paused and placed a handkerchief to his nose.

'No, sorry, the house was empty when we moved in.'

I shrugged.

'Empty? Really?'

He nodded.

'Yes, it had been empty for some time.'

A glimmer of doubt passed behind his eyes.

'Why are you so interested in our house?'

I placed a protective hand over my chest and felt my heartbeat speed up.

Fight or flight.

'I had a friend who lived up here when I was at university. Someone mentioned he might have lived in this road.'

My laugh lacked conviction and he regarded me through his spectacles like you would an ant under a microscope.

'Are you alright young man? You look very pale.'

'Yes I'm fine, I just haven't been sleeping well of late.'

His face softened.

'My wife always recommends a cup of something hot before bed. Don't you darling. Now in answer to your question, I think you should ask at the farm, they've lived here much longer than us.'

'Mmmmmuuuuch much longer,' his wife added.

I had what I needed and I nudged the gate with my leg.

It needed oiling and it creaked as it swung shut behind them. I fiddled with the latch.

'I hope you didn't think I was snooping.'

He rested a hand on the gate.

'Not at all, I hope you find out where your friend lived. Anyway, nice to meet you, and I'm glad you're settling in with your daughter. Don't forget to ask her to keep an eye out for that cat of ours.'

I waved and a smile played on my lips, although it didn't quite reach my eyes.

'I will.'

I raced back to the house, taking the steps two at time. I shut the door and leaned against the cool plaster wall. Answers were close, I could feel it in my bones.

14

I woke with a start and partially opened one eye.

Were they still here?

I sensed Amber beside me, her breathing shallow. I hadn't been with anyone special since Anna died and Amber staying over reminded me how much I missed intimacy, although even her frequent presence in my bed offered no protection against the nightmares. I cupped her warm breast in my palm. I could feel her heart beating and I wondered who the last person to touch her intimately was? We hadn't discussed our pasts, although I found it difficult to imagine she had not been romantically involved with other men.

She stirred.

'Morning.'

She moaned softly and promptly buried her head into the pillow.

'Already! I feel like I've been adrift in a lifeboat all night.'

I had to shield my eyes from the sunlight that filtered in through the blind.

'You're not the one having your sleep interrupted night after night.'

She reached over and clasped my hand.

'Sorry, that was thoughtless.'

She rolled over and lay her head on my chest, her hair the smell of sweet grass.

'You say some really weird stuff in your sleep.'

I stroked her hair.

'What weird stuff?'

'Just psychobabble. It sounded like you were fighting some kind of animal. I have no idea what goes on in that head of yours.'

'Cats,' I whispered, remembering their eyes glowing in the darkness.

Amber pinched my side, exasperated.

'Crows, now cats. How many phobias can one man have?'

The crows had thankfully not returned after Steven had suggested hanging strips of tin foil over the mirrored window.

'Maybe I need to see someone. A professional.'

She propped herself up on one elbow, revealing a perfectly shaped breast.

'Look at the deep bags under your eyes.'

I prodded gently along my cheek bone.

'Thanks for reminding me.'

'I was thinking about what Mr Royle said.'

'The house being empty when they moved in?' I replied.

'Doesn't that strike you as odd?'

Amber's breast dangled like forbidden fruit and I closed my eyes and silently counted to ten.

'There must be plenty of reasons for a house lying empty.'

Her eyes widened and she lowered her voice to a theatrical whisper.

'Maybe something happened to the previous owners?'

I pushed her away playfully.

'Come on, enough of the conspiracy theories. Now are you going in the bathroom because I need to pee.'

She slapped my bare behind as I slid out of bed.

'Off you go, age before beauty.'

'I'll be quick,' I shouted from the en suite.

Over the past months we had formulated a satisfactory living arrangement. During the week, she stayed at home with Robyn and Monty, and on Fridays and Saturdays, unless work intervened, they all stayed over: two girls, two dogs and a whole lot of fun.

I stood over the toilet and peed noisily. Out of the corner of my eye, trees bent in the wind.

'Lift the seat,' she called out.

I flushed the cistern. Last night a violent storm had blown in from the west, it slammed bins against walls, a violent, repetitive percussion that whistled and whined into the early hours. I splashed my face with cold water and peered into the shaving mirror. A haunted visage peered back. I turned to look out of the window again. In the field a flock of sheep fed voraciously, some larger ewes, too lazy to stand, balanced on their knees and nibbled the dewy grass.

But something in this idyllic picture was wrong. I grabbed the edge of the sink in alarm.

The trampoline!

Its aluminum legs lay in the grass. I ran back into the bedroom and peered through the porthole window that looked directly at the White House. There it was, wedged up against the Royles' glass conservatory.

'Fuck! Fuck!'

I threw open a drawer and grabbed some clothes. 'This is an emergency!'

Amber poked her nose out from under the duvet. 'What?'

I pointed in the direction of the White House.

'Our trampoline has sprouted wings and is over there!'

She sat up.

'Next door?'

My voice rose an octave.

'It's wedged up against their conservatory!'

She swung her legs over the side of the bed. Even with tousled hair and without make up she looked gorgeous.

'Are the girls awake?'

'I haven't heard them yet and I'm not surprised. The wind kept them awake and they were up talking well into the early hours.'

'OK, calm down.'

I hopped around, fighting with a leg of my track pants.

'I'm not feeling calm.'

Amber pulled on a t-shirt.

'Stop panicking, we can deal with it.'

'God, I hope it hasn't damaged anything, there'll be hell to pay.'

My mind imagined various unpleasant scenarios involving a large insurance claim against our un-tethered trampoline. Amber joined me at the window as the wind whipped the trees and wet leaves and debris spiralled up into black storm clouds. Amber gasped as the trampoline shifted sideways.

'Jesus. Do you think they're in?'

'I can't see any lights on.'

'Maybe they're away? Now that would be a stroke of luck.'

I opened the door and raced downstairs.

'Come on, get dressed, I'll meet you in the garage.'

The dogs barked as the electric door whirred open and like two trawlermen we stepped out into the vortex of a mini tornado. I headed out first and ran towards the White House.

'Meet me at the fence,' I shouted.

I could see a light on in the hallway, although the drive was empty. I crouched down and scurried along the front of the house to the side gate, which had access to the back garden. It wasn't padlocked and I sighed with relief as it swung open.

I sprinted head down towards the conservatory, dodging a branch as it flew past my ear. There appeared to be no superficial damage and I tried with all my might to pull the trampoline away from the structure. It was impossible, the howling wind hindered every attempt to move it and all I could do was hold on for dear life.

The force of the wind increased and it took all my strength to prevent it catapulting over the conservatory. I emptied my lungs to any god who could hear me and miraculously the wind speed ebbed a little. Ever so slowly, I edged the trampoline away from the conservatory, holding it before me like a huge shield. One step, then another.

Out of the corner of my eye I saw Amber waving her arms, at which point there was a deafening crash as a large branch fell from a nearby tree. I feared the worst, although when I looked up the branch had fallen mercifully short of their house.

I resumed the salvage operation and thankfully, for a short period of time, the wind abated.

'Stay there, we need one on each side,' I shouted across the garden.

Somehow, I manhandled the trampoline to the fence and we worked in tandem to drag it over and lay it down behind our oil tank. When we returned, the girls' faces were pressed against the kitchen window. I gave them the thumbs up and as I opened the garage door, two over-excited dogs careered past us in their frantic rush to get out into the wind-battered garden. The back door slammed shut behind us and we removed our wet clothes in the utility room. In the warmth of the kitchen we stripped to our underwear and hung our clothes in front of the Aga. The girls soon lost interest in our tale of near disaster and marched off to watch early morning TV, while Amber ran upstairs and returned with two dressing gowns.

We stood for a moment at the window, wet and exhausted, and watched the dogs chase leaves. When I turned round, Amber was smiling and then we were both laughing at the sheer madness of the last half hour. Her hair was drenched and cold rainwater dripped onto my bare arm.

'Promise me you'll tether the trampoline to something solid if another storm threatens.'

'I promise,' I said.

I felt an arm snake around my waist and she propped her dimpled chin on my shoulder. I couldn't hide the fact, as I looked at our reflection, that we looked good together. I turned and my lips brushed hers. She kissed me back, her tongue probed and a bolt of desire worked its way down through my stomach to my groin.

The kettle whistled.

'Coffee, or shall we go back to bed?'

Amber was one step ahead of me, pulling me by the arm.

'Come on, I'll race you, last one upstairs has to pay for lunch in Alderley.'

-

My mother had been itching to see the new house (and to meet Amber) and the following weekend she flew into Manchester. In a nostalgic mood and remembering happier times, I drove past Styal prison and onto the perimeter road, where the terraced houses were within touching distance of the planes landing. Like most couples, when Hope was a baby, money had been tight and we used to spend our summer holidays at my mother's cottage in the West Country: buckets and spades, candy floss and 99 cones, walks along the canal or to a picturesque cliff top pub. I liked the local beaches which were always sandy and pristine: Shaldon, Dawlish and Ness cove, which was reached by a dark, damp smugglers' tunnel cut through the cliffs. Of course, Anna had to share the lifeguard duties with mum and I knew it irritated her more than she ever admitted. It was one of my many foibles and she could never understand why I never tried to cure my phobia of water.

I pulled up behind a black taxi as two businessmen exited and stopped to watch a lady sashay across the road. She was smartly dressed in an oatmeal calf-length dress, brown boots and matching jacket. I smiled at the absurdity: she was old enough to be their mother. I beeped my horn and beckoned her over. She brushed wisps of blonde hair back under her hat as she slid into her seat.

'Punctual as ever. I wish your father had had your timekeeping gene. I might not have divorced him.'

She leaned over and kissed me on the cheek and I thought about all the shit she'd had to put up with and how grateful I was it hadn't affected our relationship. I was genuinely pleased to see her.

'Sorry it's been so long.'

'Well, I feel lucky to be here at all. Planes with propellers!'

'Propellers? I can't believe they haven't been phased out.'

'They always give me the impression that they're not going to make it off the ground, and then, when they're in the air, they get tossed around like an Airfix model.'

'Well when your stomach has settled, I've booked an excellent Thai restaurant for us all for this evening.'

'You haven't forgotten my special needs, have you?'

Mum was diagnosed as a coeliac in her 40s. No-one could work out why she was losing so much weight. That was, until she visited a specialist and she now adhered to a strict gluten-free diet.

'This ongoing dietary regime can be a bit of a chore, but it keeps me healthy.'

I turned and looked at her. She did look good and I decided it was time to indulge her a little.

'You know everyone calls you the glamorous granny.'

She squeezed my leg, clearly appreciating my attempt at flattery.

'How is Hope? I can't wait to see her. I have a few small gifts for her in my case.'

'She's talked of nothing else since I told her.'

I imagined her twitching with excitement on the school bus, the noise levels from her classmates beyond human endurance.

'What time does she get back? I want to hear all about her riding.'

'The bus drops her off at the Arts Centre around four o'clock.'

'And will Amber be coming round?'

'Yes, she can't wait to meet you. Just don't interrogate her OK?'

Mum lowered her eyes; her demure expression said it all. Butter wouldn't melt in her mouth. I frowned.

'Please?'

My mother pretended to zip up her lips.

'I promise.'

I indicated and pulled out into the one-way system and exited the airport.

'Now sit back and relax. If the traffic's good, we should be home in forty minutes.'

The A roads became country lanes and we chatted easily, even though I was aware she purposely steered the conversation away from the anniversary of Anna's death. There were still splashes of colour in the hedgerows and I was given a horticultural lesson as we drove further into the Cheshire countryside.

'You seem in a good mood,' I said.

'Didn't I tell you? I completed the sale of a small property portfolio in Florida.'

'I heard you'd been unhappy with the developers but...'

'I was, but I'm free of it all and I feel like celebrating. We turned a small profit and got out before everything went tits up. Excuse my French.'

I shrugged.

'Maybe that's the problem with buying off plan.'

Mum checked her face in the vanity mirror.

'It was not the most profitable business investment I've ever made. I'm just relieved to have finally closed the deal.'

It wasn't long before our conversation turned to the menu card, a subject she referred to as my default setting for coping with Anna.

'You know, it all reeks a little bit of a midlife crisis to me.'

I took a deep breath and tried not to rise to the bait.

'Well for the record, I'm not having a midlife crisis, and, I think I have every right to be more than a little curious.'

She rummaged in her handbag.

'Curiosity killed the cat.'

Her words took me back to her parents' garden and the high wall that kept the dead at bay. She knew she'd touched a raw nerve and we drove in silence for a minute or so. When she spoke her tone had softened.

'Tell me, did the photographs help?'

I clicked the air conditioning up, rearranging my thoughts.

'I think one of the boys may have been Robert Tyler.'

Mum nodded in agreement.

'Twig, you mean. It was such a funny nickname. Surely you must remember, he was daft as a brush.'

I shook my head.

'There was a girl. I can't put my finger on it, just something familiar about her.'

'Even after all this time? Gosh, she must have been special.'

I remembered so little really, although one thing was certain: seeing the girl in the white dress was like seeing a ghost. My mother brought me back to the present.

'And have you managed to discover who lived in this house that you talk about all the time?'

I shook my head.

'Not yet, but I did meet the current owners. They're an elderly couple who have only lived there since the mid-80s, so it's a dead end at the moment.'

'Didn't they know who lived in it before them?'

'No. They said it was empty.'

Mum pursed her lips and looked absently out of the window for a moment.

'It seems you keep running into dead ends.'

A bit like my last dream.

I braked fiercely as a traffic light turned red.

'Well without names to go with the faces, it's like trying to find a needle in a haystack.'

I looked accusingly at my mother.

'If only someone had written the names of the children on the back of the photographs.'

'Do I detect by your tone that you're blaming me for poor record keeping?'

The lights changed.

'It's not anyone's fault, it's just so frustrating.'

'Well that's OK then. You know darling, all of this was such a long time ago. I'm sure at some point we had arranged them all neatly in an album, a record of all the exotic places we visited. We weren't that incompetent you know.'

I focused on the road.

'You're right, it was a lifetime ago.'

'As the years progressed, it became evident I'd married Walter Mitty. Your father never placed a high value on photographic memories, because all the treasured memories were locked away in his head.'

Mum laughed and tapped her temple with her finger as a smile born of earlier parental fondness creased my face.

'He was a one-off, that's for sure.'

'God. You have no idea how much time I spent looking after him and clearing up his mess. It was like having a third child.'

Some faint memories came flooding back, a giant spider in the back garden, outdoor puppet shows with my sister and fishing for sticklebacks that didn't survive the journey home in jam jars.

'I remember he spent most of his life looking for things.'

'Like his car keys,' we said together.

'There was never a dull moment. Do you remember our Sunday morning game of "where has he parked the car"?'

'Usually in the middle of the front lawn.'

She got the words out before laughter erupted from her mouth and tears streamed down her face.

'Memories eh mum?'

We drove in silence for a few minutes, remembering happier times before the split.

I spoke first, my frustration showing in my voice.

'I can't explain to you what's happening to me. All I know is that I need to find out who this girl was.'

'Well, you always were an impatient soul. Couldn't wait for anything when you were younger. Saw it. Wanted it. Got it. That summed you up.'

'Mum...'

'Do you know, one Christmas we found ten pounds you'd stolen from your father's pockets.

When we asked you what you were going to do with it, you said you'd seen a Scalextric track in a magazine. You'd made your mind up, you were going to buy it and sod the consequences. I couldn't understand that side of you, it wasn't as though you were deprived.'

My mother paused and stared into the distance. I knew deep down she thought this current obsession was all related to the tragic events of a few years ago. She sighed.

'Don't let the past make you unhappy, life's too short, as we all know. I...'

She fiddled with a ring on her index finger.

'...there's something I need to share with you. I don't know why I've never told you before, it's not as though it was a secret.'

A lump formed in my throat and I swallowed uncomfortably.

'This sounds like some sort of confession.'

I sensed mum watching me out of the corner of her eye.

'It's not a confession in the strictest sense of the word. You and your sister were so young, it didn't seem necessary to involve you at the time.'

I gripped the steering wheel tightly.

'The cruise was nearly over, when something...how shall I put it, unpleasant, happened to me...'

I flinched in my seat. I instantly had visions of some sort of physical assault, or rape...

'Unpleasant! Like what?'

'Calm down and concentrate on the road. It wasn't a physical attack.'

I saw her eyes moisten.

'But it did taint an otherwise idyllic holiday.'

The tension in my hands released.

'Jesus, you had me worried…'

'Hold on, I'm going about this completely back to front. First, I need to set the scene.'

I turned my head and my eyes left the road for a split second longer than I expected. A car coming in the opposite direction swerved towards the kerb and sounded its horn as it sped past.

'Stop looking at me like that and keep your eyes on the road!'

I put both hands on the wheel.

'Sorry.'

'I want to get there in one piece. Now where was I? After we boarded the Oriana, each group of cabins had a ship's porter assigned to them. They were usually Asian men as I recall and while we went about our day, they were responsible for cleaning and changing the linen in the cabins. Our porter was a small Indian chap from Goa. He didn't speak much English but was pleasant enough, in a servile kind of way. He had a funny Indian name, but I can't remember it now. Near the end of the cruise, when we returned to our cabin to change for dinner, two personal items were missing. An expensive satin negligée I had brought especially for the cruise and…'

'Whoa, too much information.'

Mum held up her hand.

'And a ring. I'd folded the negligée up and left it under my pillow, and in the rush to get to dinner I carelessly left my jewellery by the wash basin.

'Was it your wedding ring?'

'No. I wish it had been. It was much more precious and had been passed down by my great grandmother. It was utterly irreplaceable and no amount of financial recompense could replace it.'

I felt my face tighten.

'Why did you never tell me?'

'You were just children, it didn't seem important for you to know, and then time passed. Anyway, back to the story. We had to get you and your sister ready for bed and we were late for the Captain's dinner. Your father was his usual impatient self and he made me rush. I didn't overly burden myself worrying about it that night and I certainly didn't think anything sinister had happened.'

'Did you suspect the porter?'

'Not immediately, because he helped us search for it. They got paid a pittance for their menial work and relied on the generosity of passengers at the end of the cruise to bolster their wages. Only that morning your father had left him a generous tip. In hindsight, I wish we'd kept our last American dollars. The porter had this Indian girl in England, his future fiancée if my memory serves me correctly. Perhaps the temptation had been too great for him…'

'Did you question him?'

'Your father wanted to thump him.'

'I bet he did.'

Mum looked to the heavens.

'God, what an inauspicious end to a wonderful holiday. There were cabin searches, and accusations and counter-accusations flying around the staff quarters.'

The fact that she had never spoken about this before now put my mind in a spin.

'I had no idea.'

'The ship's maintenance team even came to our cabin, dismantled the sink and checked the waste pipes to make sure I hadn't dropped it. Neither the negligée nor the ring were ever recovered and I got the distinct feeling the Bursar was pointing the finger of suspicion at your father and I for running some kind of insurance scam. It caused quite a stir amongst the other passengers.'

'I bet it did.'

'Eventually, after much hoo-ha, the porter was vindicated by the Security Officer. No evidence they said. Well, I looked him right in the eye and in my heart I knew he'd stolen it. He probably sold it in some seedy portside bar. I could see the guilt in his little beady Indian eyes.'

I imagined the porter bound to a chair being interrogated by my mother. It wasn't a pretty sight.

'It was the last day and there was no time to expect any detailed investigation. We all just wanted to say our goodbyes and get home. Well, apart from you that is.'

'Me?' I squealed in surprise.

What had I got to do with it?

My mother coughed nervously.

'You'd hidden somewhere with one of your girlfriends.'

My world tilted.

'I think you'd watched too many films about stowaways.'

A slight tremor appeared in my voice.

'Can you remember which girl?'

My mother lowered her voice to a whisper.

'You wouldn't tell us.'

She removed a bag of sweets from her handbag.

'Sherbert lemon?' she said cheerily.

I nodded and she popped one in my mouth. I sucked on the sweet thoughtfully.

Was it that simple? The girl? The dreams?

'You're very quiet all of a sudden.'

'I'm trying to take it all in.'

'If both my grandmother and mother were alive today, they would never have forgiven me. I've had to live with that awful day ever since.'

'Well at least no one died.'

'Yes, you're quite right, but I did feel so terribly guilty. I shed tears for weeks afterwards.'

Mum shook her head. I had seen her shake her head in that way so many times before, an action that expressed her disappointment in something my father had done. We drove along in silence until the next set of lights.

'What was the ring like?' I asked.

'It was the most exquisite piece. A work of art really. It was gold, topped with a unique blister pearl and inlaid with diamonds and sapphires. That wasn't all. There were rumours about the pearl's history, but sadly we'll never have the chance to find out, or indeed know its true value.'

'How did your family come by it?'

'Your great grandmother was fascinated by gemstones, especially pearls, in fact she was a bit of an authority on them. When she was alive, she would entertain me with stories about the world's most sought-after precious stones. I loved listening to her fanciful stories. Her favourite tale concerned the discovery of the famous Hope pearl in the early 19th century. It weighed an astonishing 90 grams. It was a staggering 2 x 4 inches in size and ranged in colour from greenish gold at one end to white at the other. I'll have to tell Hope about it at bedtime. Can you imagine the size of the oyster that gave birth to that baby? A hundred years ago, pearls were considerably more valuable than they are now and the pearl that found its way into our family was no exception. Nowadays, cheap imitations are two a penny.'

I put on a posh voice for effect.

'Sloane Rangers with twin set and pearls.'

Mum leant back in her seat and closed her eyes, lost in her thoughts.

'Did you know the most prestigious and sought-after pearls come from the mussel banks on the River Tay in Scotland? Their freshwater pearls are among the most beautiful and sought after in the world.'

'Did you say mussels? I thought pearls came from oysters?'

'Oysters in saltwater, mussels in freshwater.'

The story was fascinating and for a moment my own shenanigans on the Oriana were forgotten.

'I've never heard you talk about your great grandmother. Tell me about her.'

'She was called Constance. A lady with a fierce temper by all accounts. In photographs she had an uncanny resemblance to Queen Victoria and always wore the finest lace, high collars and ruffles. She married a man called George Freathy, he was a soldier, trumpeter I think. It was the custom in the early 1900s for the man to take the stone from his tie pin and have it set in a ring to give to his betrothed.'

'Should I be taking notes, because I have no idea where this story is going?'

'Well let me finish then. It was rumoured that George had been given the tie pin as a gift from one of the Regent's cousins for services to Queen and country. It was inset with a magnificent white pearl. After announcing his engagement to Constance, they took the tie pin to a jewellers, the pearl was removed and the jeweller designed an ornate gold ring for it to be set in. On the eve of their engagement party, he gave the ring to Constance as a confirmation of their undying love for each other. They were romantic buggers those Victorians. Sadly, he went off to fight in the Great War and returned years later very badly injured. He was by all accounts never the same man again.'

She took two or three long breaths.

'Constance had two children, a boy and a girl. The girl was christened Elizabeth and later became my mother. She had the trademark black hair and the skin of a southern European, which is where we get our olive skin from. She was a kind lady with the warmest brown eyes you had ever seen. Elizabeth married a jazz musician called Cyril Bushby. He sadly died of lung cancer when you were very young, in much the same way as Roy Castle.'

We passed the road sign to our village.

'Does this story have a happy ending because we're nearly home?'

'Nearly. When Constance died, the ring was passed down to my mother Elizabeth and the whole chain of events started again. I inherited it on my 18th birthday. I remember that day so well, I was so proud, we celebrated in a pub called The Artichoke in Orpington, near to where my parents lived. I had the ring valued. I can't remember exactly how many thousands of pounds it was worth back then, it seemed immaterial, because it could never be replaced. I found the original bill of sale recently while researching our family tree. It was bought by George for ten shillings, probably a king's ransom then. It was so beautiful that I never took it off. I didn't dare.'

'But you did...'

'Yes, in a moment of madness, I left it in the cabin.'

'Well, my own wild goose chase seems quite insignificant compared to the theft of Constance's pearl.'

My mother pulled a tissue from her handbag and dabbed at her eyes.

'I'm sorry, I've hardly let you get a word in edgeways. When Amber comes over, we'll put our heads together, you'll see.'

We pulled up in front of the barn.

'Well, here we are. Welcome to the Peak District.'

'What a gorgeous spot.'

I got out and opened the gate before parking in front of the garage. I carried her case up the steps and opened the front door. Within seconds, Lottie, her tail wagging from side to side like a rudder, came bounding out to greet us. My mother loved animals and instantly made a fuss of the dog,

'If you think she's excited to see you, wait until Hope gets home,' I said.

15

After we returned home from the restaurant, my mother read Hope her bedtime story. Tonight it was "The Snow Pony". The author grew up on an Australian cattle farm in Victoria and the book was about a wild horse they said could never be tamed. Hope knew the book word for word and I think she secretly dreamed of a life that mirrored the girl in the book.

Warmed by a glass of organic red wine, Amber waited patiently with the photographs and menu card. Eventually we heard footsteps and my mother's weary face appeared in the kitchen doorway.

'She's finally asleep. I wanted to tell her about the Hope pearl but she was too tired. Another time maybe.'

'It'll keep for tomorrow. If you've got any room, come and have a glass of wine and some cheese.'

I poured the deep red liquid into two glasses and asked my mother to tell Amber about the porter and the theft of items from their cabin onboard the cruise ship. By the time she'd finished talking, Amber was perched on the edge of the sofa.

'Wow, what an enthralling story, a real whodunnit, although it would appear the finger of suspicion pointed clearly at this porter chap.'

Mum raised her oval framed glasses and rubbed her eyes.

'Well who else could it have been?'

'Unless of course someone else knew it had been left there?'

'What are you suggesting Amber, that someone else had been watching the cabin? Or watching me?'

I sipped my mocktail of ginger beer and lime.

'Maybe one of dad's colourful friends crept down and helped themselves to the negligée and the ring. Maybe it was someone who wanted your underwear, and when he saw the ring, he couldn't help himself. What about that photographer chap?'

My mother sighed and kicked my leg playfully.

'You don't remember him, do you?'

'Not really, only what you've told me.'

'No, it couldn't have been Gino. He was a dear friend, who sadly is no longer with us. Honestly, men stealing underwear, that's for perverts and men in raincoats...'

'Sorry. I didn't mean to tarnish the poor man's name. Come on, let's get back to what happened that evening on the ship.'

I handed mum a plate of Époisses cheese.

'This is so moreish, I'll have to buy some in Exeter. Seriously though, we didn't have any enemies and it had to be someone with a key. Although if it was him, I never understood why he didn't take the money that was in the bedside drawer.'

'That does seem odd,' Amber shrugged and picked up the picture of the beach bar.

She pointed at the photograph.

'This place looks dreamy.'

My mother touched Amber's hand affectionately.

'We were on a stopover in Barbados, the last port of call before we headed home. A group of us had got a taxi from Bridgetown to Cobblers Cove, an exclusive hideaway with stunning views of the ocean. We had to be back at the ship by dusk, but spent a few hours relaxing and drinking banana daiquiris at a terrace bar. It was heaven. Peter and Brenda from Pinner were there, Eileen and Geoff, and another couple, but I can't remember their names now.'

Amber leant forward, her eyes shimmering in the candlelight.

'It sounds magical.'

'It was, and we all got on so well. All our cabins were on the same deck and the children spent a lot of time playing together. You've obviously heard about the E deck gang?'

Amber raised her eyebrows.

'We know all about little Casanova here.'

I dismissed Amber's frivolous comment with a wave of my hand and went to get myself a herbal tea. When I returned, Amber continued to try and tease out some connection between the events.

'Remind me again about the lady with the bandages on her legs.'

My mother sighed.

'Eileen had just recovered from cancer and an operation had left a nasty indentation on one of her legs. It must have knocked her confidence for six.'

The clock on the wall announced the arrival of midnight. Amber frowned.

'She was probably struggling to come to terms with her illness.'

'Yes, you're probably right, it's a difficult battle and you've got to be mentally strong, as I've just found out. I remember one evening not long before the ship docked in Barbados, we were involved in a lively discussion about the Watergate scandal, when she just got up and left. When dessert arrived, she reappeared. It was obvious she had been crying, her eyes were puffy and her mascara was smudged. I felt terribly guilty and tried to make peace with her, but she wouldn't have any of it, and she didn't talk to me for the rest of the evening. Luckily, the next day she was perfectly fine towards me. I think it was just one of those bad days us women have occasionally.'

My body jerked me awake. I hadn't realised I had nodded off.

'When I think about it now, it was all a storm in a teacup. Anyway, that's it, and as Gino my photographer friend told me, there's always a good story behind every photograph.'

Amber ran her finger up and down the stem of her glass.

'Did you ever see anyone afterwards?'

'Only Peter and Brenda, until they split up.'

Amber put her glass down.

'I'm sure we're going over the same ground, but do you remember anything noteworthy at all, maybe an incident involving the children?'

'Like I've said, the girls were all lovely, polite and somewhat smitten with Paul, but as for something out of the ordinary, no.'

Amber gave me a playful poke in the ribs.

'Your harem.'

The word conjured up unhealthy images of nubile maidens bathing in goats' milk and I held up my hands in mock defence.

'And you're sure none of the families lived up north?'

My mother yawned.

'I know why you're asking, and I've given it a lot of thought, but I can only remember that Peter and Brenda lived near Cambridge.'

I started clearing away the plates.

'Come on everyone, I think that's enough for tonight, I'm ready for bed.'

My mother's demure smile suggested that, for now, no more answers were forthcoming.

-

The following day, mum agreed to babysit the two girls while we popped out for a drink.

She stood at the door holding Lottie.

'It's only ten to six.'

'Early doors they call it up here,' I shouted back, as we walked to the car.

Outside, the August night was strangely muggy and a fine drizzle had started to fall. When we arrived at the pub I noticed Peter and Carol sitting tucked away in a cosy alcove. I moved to the far end of the bar, but it was too late, Peter had spotted me.

'Bloody hell, look who it is! Is it Christmas already?'

It was Peter's standard greeting for anyone who didn't drink frequently. I don't think Peter had popped in for a quick one in his life. He was the archetypal hardened drinker, stick thin with a waxy pallor. He had lost two fingers in a poultry machine accident and he beckoned us over with his damaged hand. This evening the veins in his nose stood out like angry tributaries of some great river. Peter slapped the table with his good hand, while his other hovered dangerously near Amber's rear.

'We'll join you lovebirds at the bar.'

Carol intervened.

'Be a dear and grab a couple of stools.'

We hadn't seen them socially since the welcome party and I still wondered if Peter's occasional aloofness was caused by something I'd said or done that night. I hung my coat on a hook underneath the bar.

'We're only popping in for a quick one.'

'That's what they all say, come and sit yourselves down.'

Over the next hour, pints were drunk and shorts downed. I was trying to work out why he was in such a generous mood: it was the middle of the month, so a win on the horses or the footy scores seemed a good bet. Peter's biggest love was football and it wasn't long before we started on the form of our respective teams. By 9 o'clock, only a few regulars remained at the bar and Peter was becoming louder and more opinionated as each minute ticked by. I looked across at Amber and held an imaginary phone to my ear. A few minutes later Amber reappeared at my side.

'All done?'

'I asked Janet if she wouldn't mind putting the kids to bed. She's a godsend your mum and I said we wouldn't be too much longer.'

Amber kicked my foot playfully.

'By the way, have you asked Peter about the White House yet?'

I was about to reply when Peter slapped me on the back so hard I nearly choked on my beer. His breath was sour and hoppy.

'Fancy a swim?'

'A swim? No thanks.'

Peter leant against the bar.

'You don't know about our acquisition then? Someone owed me a favour, so I took the tub off his hands.'

A hot tub! Whatever next?

Carol slid off her stool and braced herself against the bar. Like her husband, she was well oiled and behaving flirtatiously.

'You'll have to come over sometime.'

It's strange how you make irrational decisions under the influence of alcohol, how it can make you agree to things you know in the morning you are going to regret. Amber looked at me witheringly.

'We should get back...'

Peter clinked his beer bottle against mine and winked.

'So, are you missing the film industry?'

'A little. I may go back sometime, never say never, but I'm really enjoying seeing more of Hope and watching her learn to ride.'

'She'll be asking for a pony before you know it. Steven's just building stables, you could keep it at his.'

I smiled and supped my pint thoughtfully.

We'll try and hold off on the pony front for a little longer, I thought.

'I've heard you're helping out at the cricket club.'

I wiped my mouth with the back of my hand.

'News travels fast.'

Peter nodded.

'Small village you see. Shit, and someone will smell it.'

Carol thumped her husband hard on the arm.

'Language Peter...'

'The previous groundsman retired and I was approached by the chairman in the pub one night. I used to play a decent game and I thought, why not? If I get asked to play, I'll dust off my pads. If not, I'm just happy to be outdoors doing something constructive.'

Amber placed her arm round my waist.

'He's just a frustrated landscape gardener really.'

'A hidden talent eh? Still, it's a good chance to meet some new faces and get involved with the locals.'

'He's just a big kid really, Peter. It's boys' toys syndrome. You know what they say about men with large lawn mowers...'

Peter's hand lingered a little too long on Amber's arm and I felt her body tense.

'Have a go on Steven's tractor if you want to drive with the big boys.'

Amber shifted her position at the bar.

'Why don't you tell Peter about Mrs Ross?'

'Who's Mrs Ross when she's at home?'

Amber lowered her arm to my waist; it was a clear message to Peter to stay away.

'She had a close encounter, that's all I'm going to say.'

Peter nudged Carol in the ribs.

'Never been any extraterrestrial sightings along Sugar Lane before. Well, not since Mrs Dunsfold from Four Acre Farm was spotted on her annual sortie to the village in her dressing gown.'

Peter took a deep breath and belched-cum-laughed as he struggled to contain his
amusement.

'I'm sorry young man, pray, continue.'

Amber looked at her watch. I sensed she was thinking along the same lines as me. Maybe I could wind this up quickly and we could make a swift exit before the doors were locked and escape became impossible.

'It was a few weeks ago now. Steven asked me to move the trampoline so he could cut the grass in the back field. I carried it through to the front garden, where it's a little less exposed, then I went to bed and completely forgot about it.'

Peter had his drink perched precariously on his knee.

'Go on.'

'During the early hours, a vicious north westerly blew in. I slept through it, but in the morning branches were down everywhere and I looked out on to an empty front lawn. The trampoline legs were strewn to the four points of the compass, but there was no sign of it. Peter's face tightened into a look of concern.

'You and your trampoline. There's a disaster waiting to happen,'

'I found the trampoline on Steven's drive.'

Peter downed the remnants of his drink in one.

'Is that it? That's the dullest story I've ever heard!'

Carol thumped her husband hard on the arm; her frosty look told him to behave.

'A few days later, I met her husband and he asked if I could pop into the farm because his wife wanted a word. My first thought was I'd forgotten to pay my bill and I felt like a naughty schoolboy standing in her office. When she looked up from behind a pile of invoices, her smile faded and she said that in future she wanted danger money delivering milk to my house. I had no idea what she was talking about and then it clicked. She explained that the trampoline had landed directly in front of her 4x4, missing her windscreen by inches. She was shaking so much she had to sit in the cab for a while until she'd got over the shock. It was still dark and, concerned other vehicles might not see it, she dragged the trampoline into Steven's drive.'

Amber frowned.

'Luckily Mrs Ross saw the funny side. Well, eventually.'

Carol leaned forward, her breasts spilling out of her top.

'Any more mysterious tales?'

Amber arched her eyebrows.

'Well...'I stuttered.

But now wasn't the time for an alcohol induced ramble and I gathered my thoughts.

'It's not exactly a mystery and more a degree of interest in our other neighbours.'

Peter put his glass down heavily on the bar.

'You mean the White House! What do you want to know about that for?'

'Well, it's so different to the other houses in the lane. Do you know anything about its past?'

Peter leaned forward.

'You're not secretly working for a developer are you?'

'No, nothing like that, I'm just curious.'

That word again.

Carol put her mouth close to my ear.

'My mother always said curiosity killed the cat.'

Peter toyed with a pound coin.

'If you want records, you could check with the Land Registry. Or ask Carol's dad. We haven't been living back here for that long you see.'

I laughed nervously and began to wish I hadn't asked.

'I know it sounds strange, but I promise you there's nothing underhand about my enquiry.'

Peter swayed and nearly slipped off his stool.

'One more for the road?'

Carol scraped back her hair making her look even more manly than usual.

'You've met the current owners I presume. They're a little eccentric and just between you and me, they don't see eye to eye with Steven.'

Amber excused herself and disappeared towards the toilets. I edged forward.

'Something happen?'

'He built the big shed to house the cows in the winter and after it was finished, he started building the property you live in now. In both cases the Royles fought the plans because their view was being restricted. It went in front of the planning committee, then to arbitration and they lost, and that was that.'

'So there's no love lost there.'

'Frosty to say the least. They communicate, but only if they have to. We don't swap Christmas cards. Have they been stirring things up again?'

'No. They'd lost one of their cats and were asking me to look out for it. I asked them about the house and they told me they'd lived there for about twenty years.'

'If they say so. It sounds about right.'

I left Peter to devour the remaining bar snacks and focused on Carol's glazed eyes.

'I'm interested in who had the house before the Royles.'

Carol looked surprised by the admission and appeared to suddenly sober up.

'Why's that?'

'I found something from my past and it mentioned that house.'

I sensed she was about to say something when Peter hopped off his stool and broke the spell.

'Bloody hell, I need a piss. Back in a mo.'

'Did you hear that Paul's found...' but Peter was out of earshot.

'Didn't know you had connections up here. Is it family?' Carol asked.

'No. Not exactly.'

I decided it was better not to lie any more.

'The address was written on an old menu.'

Carol looked puzzled.

'Was it from a local restaurant?'

'No, it was from a cruise I went on.'

'A cruise you say? How fancy.'

'Yes. We were on a ship called the Oriana. Have you heard of it?'

'No, I can't say I have. Never been on a cruise myself. But...'

'What?'

'When was this exactly?'

'It was a long time ago. In the 1970s.'

'And you're sure it's the White House that was mentioned?'

'Yes, 100 percent.'

I sensed Carol was about to tell me something important. Then there was a deafening crash. I turned around half expecting to see Peter re-appear but he didn't. Carol looked anxiously over her shoulder and tried to conceal her embarrassment.

'I'm so sorry, can we finish this later? I'd better go and check on him. I can't explain why he does this. After one party, he hit his head on the bath. There was blood everywhere and a trip to casualty in the morning. I'd better go.'

I watched Carol reach the door and then at the last moment she turned, her face half in shadow, caught by the light from a lantern on the wall.

'What year did you say?'

'1974.'

Carol covered her mouth with her hand.

'We were all teenagers back then. Can you bring the menu card round at the weekend? I'd really like to see it.'

'I will, and thanks.'

Amber returned from the toilets. The barman was cashing up and I was the only one left at the bar.

'What's all the commotion in the car park?'

'I'll tell you about it later, come on, let's get out of here.'

-

The following evening mum flew home. It had been a thoroughly enjoyable weekend, although I sensed she was looking forward to seeing Keith and sleeping in her own bed. As I drove back home along the winding Cheshire lanes, I reflected on the events of the previous evening and my unfinished conversation with Carol. What was it she said?

We were all teenagers back then.

I collected Hope from the farm and put her to bed. Steven's daughter was proving to be a godsend and her babysitting rates were very competitive. I craved an uninterrupted night's sleep and foolishly picked up the latest nerve-jangling offering from Nicci French. It wasn't the best choice and I found the bed was no longer the warm haven it was when Amber was lying next to me. Another storm grew in strength, wind whistling round the building and fingers of light reached round the edge of the blind as the security light came on. I got up, half asleep, lifted a corner of the blind and peered out across the front garden, to the tops of swaying trees framed by black thunder clouds. I crawled back into bed and reached for a sleeping tablet. Five minutes later, my eyes closed and the book fell to the floor.

-

The ship's deck was a vast expanse of green baize interspersed with palm trees. I sat astride some sort of machine with an engine. It edged forward towards a deck area awash with children playing hopscotch and ball games. One girl in a white dress ran forward and stopped in front of me; she opened her hand and a brilliant bright light momentarily blinded me. As I reached out to touch the source of the light, a woman in a striped swimsuit appeared and attempted to wrestle the object from the girl.

'Mum let her go!' I screamed into the darkness.

She sneered back, her eyes glowing like embers, her cavernous mouth full of sharp teeth glistening with saliva. A gigantic claw cut through the air and I started to run.

Beep. beep, beep.

I fumbled in the dark, my fingers eventually finding the snooze button. It was 7.30am as I opened my eyes and focused on my breathing. Hold for one, two, three. Breathe out. I was smothered in a blanket of confusion and unease: the nightmare had changed. The girl was still there, like an irritating itch that wouldn't go away, but now the chimera had other elements. What the hell was happening to me? Was I subconsciously compensating for my failures, my marriage, my career, trying to make sense of my past, trying to make it right for once? I lay very still and forced myself to think about all the individual elements of the last few months, a complicated jigsaw, the final gaps waiting to be filled by the right pieces.

16

A day later, I caught a glimpse of a yellow sunhat through the procession of Friesian cows that ambled noisily towards the corrugated barn. I waited patiently until the column had passed and waved to the figure beyond the wall. Carol wiped her brow, dropped her trowel and met me at the paddock. I leaned casually on the gate.

'Do you remember our chat at the pub?'

'My memory hasn't gone completely.'

I looked over her shoulder.

'Is Peter around?'

'No, he's out, on another project down at Clarence Mill.'

Peter was the proverbial cat on a hot tin roof and I found it exhausting watching him rush from one job to another. I could tolerate him in small doses, while in complete contrast Carol was uncomplicated and approachable: what you saw was what you got.

'Wait there for a moment.'

I dashed back inside the house and reappeared with the menu card. Her cheeks were ruddy, flushed by her exertions and her face was streaked with black compost. We walked back to the courtyard together.

'I'd like you to look at this.'

She wiped her brow with the back of a gloved hand and when her features softened, I knew she would at least give my story a fair hearing.

'So, this is what all the fuss is about. You know I'd been thinking about what you said...'

We walked over to a small ornamental table. My heart was in my mouth and I felt a nervous cramp take hold of my stomach.

'I know this might sound utterly ridiculous, but ever since we moved up here things have happened that I can't explain.'

Her eyes were pools of liquid comfort and the tension began to lift from my shoulders.

'Let's see if I can help. Do you want a cold drink?'

'I'm fine thanks.'

She took her gloves off and sat down.

'So, tell me what all this is about?'

I placed the card on the table and took a deep breath.

'This all sounds a little absurd, but here goes.'

She looked up at me and smiled warmly.

'I'm sure it's not absurd at all.'

'When we moved up here from London, I found this menu in an old chest. It's from a cruise my family went on in 1974.'

I moved the menu card round so she could see it properly.

'Let me get my glasses.'

She returned from the kitchen and studied the front cover.

'My, you were lucky. Long time ago though.'

'Yes it was.'

I opened the card and she read the more legible messages.

She frowned.

'I still don't understand why you're interested in our neighbours?'

I drew her attention to the lower right-hand corner.

'Look.'

She peered incredulously at the faded words.

'Well I never! I told Peter about your discovery and he thought you were making it up.'

She patted my arm like you would a small dog. I was a bundle of nervous energy, I couldn't keep my hands still. In the old days a cigarette would have calmed me and I would have killed for one right now.

'I couldn't believe it myself, coincidences like this happen to other people, don't they? I haven't a clue who wrote it because there are no names paired with the address.'

Carol ran a calloused forefinger over the words.

'Although there is a phone number,' I pointed out.

She leaned back and her eyes sparkled.

'And you want to find out who wrote this?'

'I do.'

I held my breath and waited.

She smiled and revealed two badly chipped front teeth.

'72007. I recognise that number like it was yesterday.'

I gasped.

'Really?'

'We used to phone it all the time.'

My insides churned.

'You mean you know who lived in the house?'

'Of course I do, why didn't you ask me before?'

'Well, it didn't seem appropriate before, because I didn't really know you.'

'We don't bite.'

I put my head in my hands.

'I know, I know.'

'If you'd asked earlier, we could have solved your mystery without any mithering. It was the Keens.'

I felt lightheaded, giddy.

'Did they have children?'

Carol laughed.

'We used to play together. Three bonny girls, although we haven't seen them in ages, but...'

My skin prickled.

'What are their names?'

The names rolled off her tongue.

'Suzanne, Julie and Sara. And their older brother, Stephen.'

Carol raised an eyebrow.

'You know them?'

The words caught in my throat.

'I think I did.'

She took my arm.

'Do you want a glass of water?'

'No, honestly, I'm fine. Could you tell me more about them?'

'Their father was a salesman for a drinks company. He liked a tipple, just like ours. His wife, Eileen, was a homely woman, but I'm sure you'd rather hear about the girls?'

I straightened up and turned to face her. I felt like I held the winning numbers on a lottery ticket.

'Hold on.'

I turned the card over and there were Geoff and Eileen's names. I hadn't meant to interrupt and I sat down and encouraged her to continue. She placed her hands either side of the menu card, took a breath and continued.

'I remember the Keens telling us about a holiday they were going on. You were all privileged kids to go to the...where did you say, the Caribbean? Well, it must have cost Mr Keen an arm and a leg, for all five of them. They were like us, comfortable but not rich folks you see. Sadly, our father never saw eye to eye with Mr Keen. He was a bit of a ladies' man back then and he had a bit of a reputation in the village. I don't think his wife had a clue where he was most of the time. That didn't affect us children, we all played together here in these fields, Steven and I being similar ages 'an all. We used to play tig round the farm, or at harvest time we'd play on the hay bales in the top field. Well, until one of the girls fell off and broke her ankle. You could hear the scream in Buxton. I remember Mrs Keen gave us a right telling off. My mother thought she was a little neurotic because she wanted her girls to be perfect. Overly protective some folks said, protecting them from all the bad things in the world.'

Carol looked up at some passing clouds.

'Penny for them, 'I said, although my mind was thinking about something my mother had said. Carol had a distant look in her eyes.

'Just a pleasant memory. Those boys were a handful, and they used to drive our mothers mad. "Steven!" our mums would scream from their back doors. The boys would always turn up at the wrong house, just to irritate them. Same names you see, but they were like chalk and cheese those two. I haven't seen Stephen Keen for a long, long time. I believe he married an Australian girl and lives in Sydney.'

Carol paused, as if she wasn't sure whether to continue. My heart beat faster and I placed my hands in my lap so Carol couldn't see them shake.

'I think my parents knew them.'

Carol nodded.

'It's a small world all right. Look, no matter what people said back then, they were a good family. Bring them pictures over, I'd like to see them. Oh, and Peter's going to have to eat his words...'

A tight knot formed in my stomach as I prepared to ask the next question.

'What was Suzanne like?'

'She was a looker that one. Her parents wanted her to be a model or dancer or sommat.'

'A model, yes I'd heard that,' and then I lowered my voice.

'I think Suzanne and I were more than friends.'

Carol whistled softly.

'Oh my, this is a juicy tale. You had good eye, she was an angel to look at. Then something happened to her and she became quite wild and unruly. I think she rebelled against all the pressure they put on her.'

Carol clapped her hands.

'It seems we've solved your little mystery, maybe you'll have some peaceful nights now. I know what it's like when you can't sleep. Peter snores something rotten and I have to use ear plugs.'

I became distracted and Carol's voice became fainter and fainter.

'...and plenty of frolics in the hay. They was happy times back then.'

Carol waved her hand in front of my face.

'Hello? Paul?'

A look of fear hardened my features.

'Did something happen to Suzanne? An accident maybe?'

Carol looked confused.

'That's a strange question. Why do you ask?'

A drawn-out sigh escaped my lips.

'Well it might explain everything.'

'The girls are alive and well, and occasionally we see Mrs Keen. She beat the cancer but…sadly the same can't be said of her husband.'

I froze.

'Why, what happened to him?

Carol stood up.

'Come inside, I've got a casserole I need to check on.'

A delicious tang of earthy flavours hit me from the range and Carol invited me to join her on a small bleached wooden pew. Her face was inches from mine.

'Well this is where it gets weird. Mr Keen disappeared. It was the talk of the village for years…rumours started about business debts and affairs. Shortly afterwards, the house was sold to a local developer and Mrs Keen moved out west with the girls. The developers planned to knock it down, but the plans were rejected and the house remained empty until the Royles bought it. I felt so sorry for those poor girls and it seemed to affect Suzanne more than the others. As I said before, she changed. She was very close to her father you see.'

Goose bumps ran up my spine. It was like a TV drama. Carol picked a dead leaf from a plant in the centre of the table.

'Maybe he's dead, maybe he's living a secret life with another woman, or disappeared like Ronnie Biggs or Lord Lucan. Maybe he's back in the Caribbean…'

Carol shrugged her shoulders. I sat in silence for a moment and watched her tidy the table. Never in my wildest dreams had I expected to stumble upon a story like this. She turned from the sink with a brooding look in her eyes.

'But if he is out there, he could never come back here.'

17

The next morning, I sat in the kitchen and stared out past the farm, toward the hazy hills of the Peak District National Park. Today was the third anniversary of Anna's death and I had slept fitfully as my mind dragged me back again to the past; I felt like every ounce of energy had been sapped from my body. I kicked back my chair and decided there was only one person who could lift my spirits.

An hour later, the doorbell rang.

I caught a glimpse of myself in the hallway mirror, my forehead creased with worry lines and there were dark hollows beneath my eyes. For a second, I struggled to recognise my own reflection.

I opened the front door.

'Thanks for coming round.'

Amber's blue eyes were shimmering pools of sympathy and my whole body wilted as she wrapped her arms around me.

'It's going to be OK.'

I spoke into her hair. It smelled of honey.

'This whole affair is beginning to exert some strange pull over me and I don't where it's all going to end. I thought after speaking to Carol I might have found some peace.'

Amber caressed my head.

'Your mind is overflowing with conflicting emotions at the moment. Sit down and tell me exactly what Carol said.'

I somewhat reluctantly began to recount the previous day's events. When I'd finished, Amber clapped her hands together.

'Well I'll be damned. It all adds up, the photographs, the dreams, the girl who was so in love with you, that she scrawled her address and telephone number, hoping you might keep in touch…'

I felt like I was in a fishbowl, watching the world through a distorted lens. I should have felt elated, but I didn't.

'It doesn't feel like that to me.'

She followed me to the window and held my head in her hands.

'It's all over, case closed as they say in the movies. Leave it to drift away.'

I remained at the window, watching the sheep play king of the castle on a small hillock.

'Not quite,' I whispered.

She turned towards me, her mouth gaping open.

'You're not thinking about meeting her?'

I didn't want her to see the steely determination in my eyes and looked away. She prodded me in the ribs with more force than I expected.

'Unless of course you have some unfinished business…?'

My head felt like it was about to explode and I gripped the back of a chair.

'I wish I'd never heard of the Keens. I wish I'd thrown the bloody thing away.'

Amber held my hands and her features softened.

'Let me play devil's advocate for a moment. What if you hadn't moved up north? Who's to say who you might have tracked down? You might have met some gangster's moll from Essex because it sounds like your parents were mixing with some colourful characters.'

My resistance weakened and I let Amber talk me down off the ledge.

'I want you to know I don't make a habit of searching for old girlfriends. I've never even been on Friends Reunited.'

'I should hope not. Look, even I took a peep recently.'

'Really? Who were you looking for?'

'I'm not telling you about my dark past.'

I felt myself wading through quicksand again.

'I doubt it's as dark as mine.'

Amber lowered her gaze.

'Sorry, I didn't mean it like that. I can't begin to imagine what mental anguish you've been going through lately.'

I fiddled nervously with a set of keys as I thought about what I was about to say next.

'I haven't told you everything.'

She flopped into a battered armchair.

'You mean there's more?'

'Sometime after the cruise, Mr Keen disappeared. He left one morning and never returned and Mrs Keen and her daughters moved away soon afterwards.'

She shuffled to the edge of her seat.

'A sixth sense told me this was about more than just coincidences.'

I held up my hand.

'Wait, there's more. Mrs Keen occasionally visits Carol's mother right here at the farm. Look I don't want to go unearthing old skeletons, but...'

Amber cut in, although her reply was guarded.

'But what, exactly?'

I couldn't believe what I was about to say. I felt like I had inhaled a powerful drug that wouldn't let me go.

'Whether it's fate, destiny, providence, whatever word you want to use, I need to meet her.'

She looked at me incredulously.

'If you don't mind me asking, what are you and an old lady you haven't seen for 30 years going to talk about?'

I ran a hand over my chin, I hadn't shaved for a few days and my palm rasped over the stubble.

'Ever since I found the menu card, I've been bombarded with images of a girl who looks remarkably similar to her daughter. And I want to know why.'

'We've been over and over this. Maybe the menu card triggered something in your subconscious, a suppressed memory. It can happen you know.'

The hairs on the back of my neck stood up.

'You still think something happened on the cruise and I buried it for all these years?'

Amber got up and paced the room.

'Excluding your mother's catastrophe, I'm sure if it had been something really awful you might have heard about it before now.'

'Carol told me Suzanne was married, but had never had children, although her eyes suggested she may have suffered some hardship.'

'There you go, everyone has to deal with adversity, there's nothing sinister about that. Do you really want to know what I think?'

Amber stopped. She folded her arms and looked hard at me.

'I think you've become so obsessed with this whole Suzanne thing that you're clutching at straws. You found out what you wanted to know, now get on with your life.'

There was a long pause.

'Well?'

I thought of the countless times I had lain awake dissecting every thread, every facet of the dream, trying to make sense of it all.

'I hear what you're saying but these dreams transported me back to the ship. Why is that?'

'They're just dreams, we all have them.'

'Is it normal to have so many terrifying dreams about one person? Come on, help me out here, where's your support gone all of a sudden?'

She knelt in front of the chair, her eyes found mine.

'There's usually a simple, rational explanation, but if it'd make you feel better, perhaps you should go and visit a psychic or an expert on dream interpretation.'

'Do you honestly think it would help?'

'It might. I saw an interesting programme about people who suppressed dormant memories, usually severe emotional trauma. Now I'm not saying you suffered anything like that, but these fragments of information you're experiencing may be part of a more traumatic memory. A memory your mind has filed away in a part of your brain that is out of reach. My mother visited a clairvoyant once and found out...'

I cut her off in mid-sentence.

'Maybe I will go and see one of these dream specialists, but my mind is made up, I'm going to meet Mrs Keen.'

We remained silent for a while, each of us thinking about what the other had said, neither willing to give an inch. I felt it was a pivotal moment for our relationship. I wasn't expecting her eyes to fill with tears.

'I care deeply for you, and I can't stop you meeting her, but please tread carefully, OK?'

She looked past me, distracted for a moment.

'There's something else isn't there?' I asked, sensing things between us were still not quite right.

She wiped her eyes.

'We seem to be drifting.'

'Are we?'

She shook her head.

'Sometimes I look at you and I don't see the man I met at the school gate. This whole affair has changed you. It's begun to take over your entire life.'

She looked for a response in my eyes. I bit my lip; I didn't want to fight.

'I'm sorry, forgive me.'

She moved towards me, pressed her warm body against mine. I closed my eyes and breathed in her fragrance.

'Please cut me a little slack. I was always understanding when you had projects on. I'll organise a babysitter and we'll go out for a meal, some wine, some…'

She placed a finger against my lips.

'I want you to be normal again, and by the way that's the lamest apology I've ever heard. A meal, wine and some quality time in your bed would be the least I deserve. I'll agree to a truce, but only if you promise not to talk about you know who. Let's give her a rest for a while. Promise?'

I kissed her.

'I promise,' I lied.

18

I was roused from my desk by a loud knock at the back door. I peered out and saw Carol's wind-blown face pressed to the glass. I opened it and she blustered into the room with a flurry of leaves.

'She's coming!'

It took a few seconds for the words to sink in.

'Mrs Keen?'

'Two o'clock this afternoon. I've not told her too much, although I've prepared her for a surprise.'

I gathered myself, bent forward and kissed her on the cheek.

Carol blushed.

'You're an angel, I'll be there.'

As I watched her fight her way back across the paddock, something unpleasant stirred in my gut. I knew what it was as I had felt it before: I was genuinely frightened what I might discover.

-

Self-doubt seeped imperceptibly through every fibre of my body and I contemplated turning back. What was I doing with this bundle of old memories tucked under my arm? What was I doing looking to a complete stranger for answers?

I reached the gate. One small step at a time.

Carol appeared, a smudge of make-up round her eyes, gesturing to a table in a sheltered corner of the courtyard where a frail woman sat. I pretended this was all perfectly normal.

'Hello Mrs Keen. It's a pleasure to meet you. I believe Carol's told you some, if not all, of my story.'

A shrivelled, sinewy hand extended from the sleeve of a pale blue dress.

'She has indeed. I believe you're originally from London. So how are you enjoying the rural life in Cheshire?'

I gestured to the surrounding hills.

'You only have to look around...'

Mrs Keen smiled sweetly and allowed her eyes to gaze wistfully into the distance.

'It's exactly what drew us here all those years ago. And your children?'

My heart rate slowed a little.

'I only have one and Hope has settled into her new school and she loves living near the farm.'

I held my breath for one, two, three and waited for Mrs Keen to ask me about Hope's mother.

'It's so important isn't it for the children to be happy. I think as parents we can cope with most things life throws at us, but upheaval and change of circumstance are never easy for young children. Now Carol's told me a little about your fascinating story, so now I'm here, please tell me more.'

I breathed out and began to relax. This old lady may actually be an ally.

'I must say, standing here in front of you, my story seems a little trivial, a little less earth shattering. I hope you're not going to be disappointed.'

'Nonsense, I understand your rationale completely. Carol's probably told you we used to live in the White House.'

Her bony hand pointed down the lane.

'She has.'

Was I mistaken or did her milky eyes register a glimmer of recognition?

'And it would appear we have something in common?'

Carol and her mother appeared with a tray laden with afternoon tea.

'Here we are ladies. Sorry, and Paul.'

'Tea? Sugar? I'm glad that wind has dropped.'

I sat myself in between Mrs Keen and Carol. The old lady moved her cane and hooked it on the end of the table.

'Carol said you have something to show me?'

I reached into the folder and removed the well-thumbed menu card. Mrs Keen regarded the picture of the ship and a nostalgic sigh slipped from her thin lips.

'Go on, open it, have a look inside.'

She perched her reading glasses on the bridge of her nose and scrutinised the scrawled messages with great care. Occasionally she looked skywards, like she was praying.

'Well I never...Tell me again how you came by it?'

'It was a fluke. It'd been hidden at the bottom of an old chest.'

Mrs Keen didn't reply immediately, choosing instead to stare at a flock of birds as they descended noisily into the branches of a nearby tree. I guided her eyes to the left-hand corner.

'Imagine my amazement when I discovered this. I think you might recognise the address.'

Mrs Keen peered through her glasses.

'It's true, that is our address. How truly astonishing, it takes me back, it really does.'

My hand brushed against hers.

'Do you believe in fate?'

Mrs Keen looked at Carol's mother.

'I think I might.'

'Then you can imagine how I felt when I moved into the house next door.'

'It certainly is an amazing coincidence, a chance in a million I'd say.'

I turned the card over.

'And here, you and your husband have signed the card.'

'Oh my word! Look Carol!'

For a fraction of a second I glimpsed a hint of understanding in her anguished eyes. I couldn't explain it, but somehow she knew I had also suffered the loss of someone close. Her mood altered as we drank our tea and she became more reflective.

'My poor husband.'

'God rest his soul,' Carol's mother whispered under her breath.

We sipped our tea in silence, each of us deep in our own thoughts, then a semblance of serenity returned to her face and the awkward moment passed.

'Sadly, I don't remember the holiday very well. The girls occasionally talked about it when they were younger, although I've not heard it brought up in conversation for many years now. Carol also mentioned something about photographs?'

'I have them right here.'

I shook the folder and the photographs dropped on to the table. Mrs Keen picked up the picture of the E deck gang. I touched her skeletal arm, the translucent skin stretched tight over blue veins and bright bone.

'I think you might recognise some of the children.'

'Oh my, look at this happy bunch, and you all look so smart! I can't say I remember. No, wait, that's my Suzanne sitting on the end of the sofa. She was a pretty young thing back then, had all the boys running after her.'

I held my breath. Did she know? If she did, she wasn't letting on.

Mrs Keen nudged her glasses down onto the bridge of her nose.

'Are you in this photo?'

'Sadly I'm not. Maybe I took it.'

A toothless, half-smile creased her cheek when I placed the photograph of the two older boys alongside the one of the E deck gang.

'I have more, but I'm sure you don't want to see me dressed as a 70s pop star.'

'Oh lord' she exclaimed after a moment's scrutiny, 'look, it's our Stephen. Gosh, he was a tall lad. Who is the other boy?'

'I think it's a boy called Twig.'

'What an unusual name.'

'It wasn't his real name, it was a nickname. We think his real name was Rob Tyler.'

Mrs Keen slowly shook her wizened head.

'Sorry, I don't remember, although it's wonderfully nostalgic to look back at these old photographs. We were very lucky to travel to all these fantastic places, especially when most of our friends were just taking package holidays to Spain. I suppose this leaves me with a question for you.'

I knew what she was about to ask me.

'Would you like me to tell the girls?'

A meeting.

It was too mind-boggling and preposterous to comprehend. The words wouldn't come and I nodded instead, as fear and guilt scrambled my thought processes and tightened my throat. She turned to Carol's mother.

'Do you remember the boys playing Cowboys and Indians around the farm?'

'Right little monkeys they were, especially those two Stephens!' Carol's mother replied.

I coughed self-consciously. I felt like a serene swan gliding effortlessly on the surface of a lake, while its legs paddled frantically under the surface. Mrs Keen took a delicate sip of tea.

'Tell me what you want me to do.'

I held my breath. Stick or twist. I exhaled.

'Do you think they'd come?'

'I can only ask them. I'll get a message to Carol once I've spoken with them.'

Carol pinched my cheek playfully.

'I'm sure they'll be dying to meet you. Good looking man like you…'

Mrs Keen checked her watch.

'Oh lord, look at the time. I have another engagement this afternoon. Can you call me a taxi? I need to be somewhere by three.'

Carol turned and headed back towards the house.

'I'll do it right away.'

Mrs Keen looked down as if she had forgotten something.

'How rude of me, do you have any pictures of your parents? I can't place them, but then my memory is not what it used to be.'

I rummaged in the folder for the doctored photo. Mrs Keen studied the faded, sepia image.

'I remember where this was. It was Antigua. No it wasn't. Oh, let me think. That's Cobblers Cove in Barbados. What a lovely place. Who are the other couple?'

'They're my parents.'

Mrs Keen squinted at the polaroid.

'What was your mother's name?'

'Janet.'

Her tone became curt.

'Janet you say. No, it doesn't ring a bell.'

A tractor rumbled past and we waited for it to disappear before resuming our conversation.

'Well, let's not dwell on the past.'

I felt I was being dismissed and I looked across at Carol, who had reappeared from the kitchen. In the end, nothing more was said and Mrs Keen raised herself awkwardly from her seat with the help of her stick.

'Let's not leave on a sad note, life must go on. It's been a very pleasant afternoon and thank you for bringing back...' she paused, '...some happy family memories.'

I kissed her bony cheek.

'It's been lovely meeting you.'

A tinge of colour flushed her cheeks.

'I can't promise anything, but when I get a chance, I will speak to the girls and tell them all about you.'

As she limped towards the kitchen door, I couldn't help looking down at her leg, the concave dip, proof that she was indeed the lady my mother had met all those years ago on the Oriana.

19

That evening, I scrolled through my phone's address book. I had a burning question I needed an answer to. My mother answered on the third ring.

'Hi Mum, it's me.'

'You don't need to introduce yourself every time you call, I do recognise the voice of my only son.'

'Habit unfortunately. Listen, I've been itching to tell you about what happened today.'

'By the tone of your voice I presume this has something to do with the cruise. Goodness, you've been like a dog looking for a bone.'

'You might want to sit down.'

'I am. Now come on, tell me who you met that has you in a fluster.'

'Well, you'll never believe it but...Mrs Keen.'

Maybe I imagined it, but I was sure I heard a note of irritation in her voice.

'Well, what a small world, and was her husband with her?'

'No he wasn't, and what I'm about to tell you might come as a bit of a shock.'

'I'm not sure anything can shock me anymore.'

'He disappeared not long after the cruise.'

I wish I could have seen her mask slip.

'How awful.'

'There's never been any closure.'

Mum cleared her throat.

'It's very sad when these things happen. As I get older it seems to be one funeral after another.'

I burrowed deeper, looking for a reaction.

'It was the talk of the village and there were rumours that he ran off with another woman. It turned out Mr Keen was a bit of a dark horse.'

I heard my mother sigh.

'My what a tangled web you've uncovered.'

'Yes, curiosity certainly killed this cat.'

Mum laughed halfheartedly at my jocular remark. We were playing cat and mouse and she knew it.

'That poor, poor family, it must be terribly difficult to come to terms with something like that. Then again, when I was divorcing your father, I always hoped he might just disappear!'

My irritation rose and I clasped the phone tightly.

'This is hardly the time for frivolous comments like that.'

Her voice softened.

'You're right. Now tell me more about your meeting.'

My self-control wavered and I closed my eyes. Breath in, hold it. One, two, three and out.

'I expected her to be surly and prudish, but she was polite and charming. When I showed her the photographs, she seemed genuinely excited when she recognised Suzanne and her son Stephen. He moved abroad and I sensed she misses him.'

'Where does he live now?'

'Sydney, I think.'

'So you won't be meeting him then.'

She paused.

'Did she remember you?'

'I don't think so, but I could tell by the way she listened to me that she was intrigued by my story.'

'And how was her leg? I kept telling her to have reconstructive surgery on it but she wouldn't listen to me.'

'She has to walk with a stick.'

'Poor thing.'

I spread the photographs out in front of me.

'After I showed her the photograph of Cobblers Cove, I asked her if she remembered you.'

The phone buzzed with interference.

'And then something strange happened.'

My mother sounded puzzled.

'What do you mean?'

'I'd say there was an underlying sense of bête noire...'

The other end of the phone fell silent.

'Are you still there?'

'Yes, yes I'm still here, just odd thoughts wriggling around in my head. What were you saying?'

I clenched my fists in frustration: I wanted to yell down the phone.

'I found that strange because I thought you said you spent a lot of time together on the ship.'

Her tone soured.

'We weren't joined at the hip, maybe the radiotherapy addled her brain.'

A question lay unspoken on my lips.

'Are you sure nothing happened between you?'

'Is this some sort of interrogation?'

We were jousting and I had pierced her amour with a direct hit.

'No, of course not.'

I imagined her elegant hand raised in the air as she brushed me off.

'There were hundreds of couples on that ship and maybe I didn't stand out like some of the more colourful characters. I'm surprised she didn't remember your father. God, his antics were way past what was classed as acceptable. He spent most evenings cavorting round the ball room like a mad bull. If memory serves me, her husband was also involved in the hilarious Swan Lake ballet. Most nights, your father, Barfield and Mr Keen were last to leave the bar. So, what now?'

I paused momentarily for effect.

'Not quite sure. Mrs Keen is going to speak to her daughters.'

There was a note of caution in her reply.

'I hope you know what you're doing.'

I wasn't sure I did and imagined Mrs Keen phoning her daughters and explaining that she had recently met a slightly eccentric man who had found an old menu from a cruise his family went on in 1974. He's spent the last six months on some sort of crusade to find you, because it appears, thirty years ago, you wrote declarations of undying love to him. My voice faltered and lacked conviction.

'If I don't, I might always wonder what if…'

My mother was like a white shark and she could smell blood in the water from hundreds of miles away as she homed in on my weak point.

'Well if you meet this Suzanne, I hope she doesn't tell you something you don't want to hear.'

I stammered, taken aback by her directness.

'What do you mean?'

She was lining up for a kill.

'History is littered with stories of teenage romances and spurned love and they usually have unhappy endings.'

The skin on my neck prickled and anger rose to the surface.

'Well that's definitely not my motive.'

Her words bristled with animosity.

'I've told you what I think, let's leave it at that.'

I bit my tongue. She had made it perfectly clear that she felt I was on a wild goose chase and my dreams were all connected to the tragedy that befell Anna. Having pushed me a little too far, her cheery tone suddenly returned: she was like Jekyll and Hyde.

'Golly, all this talk of old girlfriends and I forgot to ask you how Amber is?'

I unintentionally chewed the inside of my cheek, and winced as I spoke.

'She's fine, but very busy with her agency at the moment. Things can get quite complicated between us, juggling the girls and two dogs.'

'She's a very strong and highly motivated young woman and I take my hat off to anyone who's brought up a child on their own and started a company without the support of a husband.'

'She's witty, clever and a great mother and I'm very lucky she didn't drop me like a hot potato once she saw I was damaged goods.'

'Even so, do I detect a gradual cooling of your relationship?'

She was walking on thin ice. I pushed back my shoulders and straightened my posture in an attempt to reclaim my authority.

'For the record: no comment.'

It was none of her business and it was my turn to be economical with the truth. After the call ended, I sat quietly in an old rocking chair by the window. I concentrated on the motion, de-cluttering my mind, allowing a new chain of thought to surface. I remembered Amber had described a television programme she'd seen where a Polish girl had completely erased the fact that her father had murdered her mother, even though she witnessed the terrible crime. Twenty years later, a Polish phrase uttered by a patient in a hospital, a complete stranger, brought that haunting night back to her. The journalist explained that it was the same word her Polish mother had screamed as she was killed by her husband. The story however, ended tragically, when the grief-stricken girl hung herself. I placed my foot on the floor and stopped the chair. This was not the direction I wanted my thoughts to travel in. Was it possible I had a dormant memory waiting to be freed? Something significant I had purposely suppressed? And if this was the case, maybe I just needed the right key to unlock it?

20

Lush green fields stretched into the distance as far as the eye could see, and above, the sky was a deep cobalt blue. Mrs Keen had been true to her word and I stood on the threshold waiting to make my entrance.

After hours of soul-searching, I now believed this reunion and what it would reveal was meant to be. It was my destiny. Today, Julie and Sara had made the journey back to the farm where they spent so much time as children. Sadly, one important person was missing. I walked past the door to the kitchen into the sheltered courtyard, to the same table where I had met Mrs Keen.

As I approached the table the two women stood up. Carol made the introductions and I exchanged pleasantries with them. The initial atmosphere was cordial, if not slightly awkward. As I began to tell the story for what seemed the hundredth time, I felt self-conscious, like I was pitching a film trailer to a producer.

To their credit, they listened courteously without interrupting, but there was little in their facial expressions that put me at ease. I skipped over the mundane, kept the narrative concise, hopefully gripping. However, when I paused for breath halfway through, I saw not a flicker of empathy in their eyes.

When I finished talking, a gust of wind eddied round the courtyard and Julie brushed strands of fine hair away from her face. She took a step forward, her arms crossed defensively across her chest.

'Are you trying to contact all the girls who signed the card?'

Her tone was unexpectedly barbed and my heart sank like a stone dropped into a deep well.

So much for diplomacy.

If this had been a boxing match, she just won with a KO. Reeling from the accusation, all I wanted to do was turn and run, but self-preservation kicked in and I tried to salvage a modicum of integrity. I spoke slowly and clearly, my voice showing not a hint of emotion.

'Of course not.'

Julie looked away, disinterested. She was about my height, with mousy hair, a touch of eyeshadow and a smear of lipstick. She was not someone who would turn my head if we passed in the street. Her voice had a thick northern inflection.

'Well, I told mum that everyone's doing this kind of thing now, disenchanted men and women contacting old school mates in the hope of igniting old passions.'

Her sister nodded in agreement. I was utterly speechless. Julie obviously had her own agenda and she made me feel like a predatory male caught with his trousers down. I looked across to Carol for support; she was standing nearby dead-heading a plant. I could tell she was clearly embarrassed by Julie's frosty rebukes. I decided to regroup and ward off her cross-examination.

'If the shoe had been on the other foot, wouldn't you have done the same?'

Julie shrugged her shoulders.

'You've got this all wrong. I'm not some sad man with relationship issues, that's absurd. There was no pre-meditation, no plan. I just found an old menu signed by some children a long, long time ago, and…well I was intrigued by the coincidences.'

Julie looked down at her feet. I'd evidently touched a raw nerve, crossed some sort of invisible line and I wasn't doing myself any favours reminding them of painful family memories. I looked to Carol for guidance on how to break the uncomfortable silence and diffuse the air of tension. Carol walked over.

'I think we've all started off on the wrong foot here. Come and look at the card, I think Paul has every right to be curious, goodness it's an unbelievable twist of fate, don't you think?'

The ladies exchanged stoical glances. Her younger sister was still yet to speak.

'Did you try and trace any of the other children?'

Julie flicked her hair away from her face and I was reminded of a horse keeping flies away.

'No,' I pleaded, 'please, hear me out. I'm not having a midlife crisis and I'm not using the premise of any past friendship as a tool for rekindling relationships. Please, believe me, that was never my intention.'

The women whispered conspiratorially and I prepared myself for a fresh onslaught and searching questions about my marital status. A last nod to her sister and Julie turned back, seemingly appeased for the moment.

'Can we see the menu?'

At last, a modicum of interest and a hint of a smile. Carol joined us round the table and opened the card.

'I knew that number by heart. Phones were so new back then, we were always calling you and mum used to get so angry and threaten to put a lock on it.'

Julie smiled at Carol, obviously remembering happier times.

'It really is our old number.'

I read out the messages, mimicking children's voices and gradually the atmosphere mellowed.

"To gorgeous Paul, lots of love Suzanne xxxxxxxx"

"To Paul, All my love Julie xxxxx"

Julie looked up at her sister.

'I can't lie Sara, it's our handwriting.'

I placed a hand on the table.

'You see, I wasn't making it up. These were probably written on the last night.'

Julie turned the card over and tugged on her sister's arm.

'Oh my God! I remember Martine, she was the girl who was brilliant at table tennis.'

As I stepped back from the table, Sara spoke for the first time. She had very thin lips and her voice was rounded, her vowels polished, unlike her sister.

'You were popular with the girls then.'

I shrugged my shoulders self-consciously. The evidence was irrefutable, there in black and white. Julie frowned.

'Well it seems it's true, we were all on the cruise together, although I can honestly say hand on heart I have no recollection of you or this gang we were supposed to be part of.'

Out of the corner of my eye I could see Carol thinking, why are you being so rude?

For a minute the girls talked amongst themselves.

'I remember Martine, but …' Julie giggled, '...the rest I find all a little embarrassing. We were just teenage girls back then and Suzanne was a hopeless romantic. She was very different to us.'

I cleared my throat.

'Look, I don't want to make a big deal about this, I understand this all took place a long time ago...' my voice trailed off, unconvincingly.

'Sara will back me up, she knows what Suzanne was like.'

Sara had an oval face framed by blondish hair and when she spoke her lips hardly moved.

'Suzanne was precocious, always a bit of a flirt. We don't see her much now.'

I was surprised by her brusqueness because Mrs Keen had given me the impression the girls were all close. I stepped back. There was something else going on here and then it hit me. There was a definite undercurrent of jealousy. My reply was measured.

'I understand your reaction, we've all changed since we first met on the Oriana but...'

Julie cut me off.

'I think what's in the past should stay in the past.'

My strategy hadn't worked and with not a hint of an apology for her earlier viper-like attack, our conversation ended. It was evident empathy and compassion were not traits that sat easily on Julie Keen's shoulders.

'When I'd played out this meeting in my mind, this was not what I envisaged. I came here today full of good intentions, hoping to recall a special time in our lives. Hoping for answers.'

The stark truth was, we did not remember each other and had nothing in common. I wanted to show them the photographs and tell them how many sleepless nights I'd had dreaming about their sister, but now I felt hurt and deflated and I kept them in my pocket. Julie came over to shake my hand but her handshake was limp and lifeless, like her hair.

'We need to go. We appreciate you showing us the menu card and I hope you don't feel you've wasted your time.'

Then as an afterthought.

'Maybe you should frame it?'

I was unsure if she was being sincere or sarcastic. However, not to be goaded, I forced my lips into a thin smile.

'Yes, maybe I will.'

Julie collected a box of vegetables from a trestle table near the back door while I picked up the folder and stood awkwardly waiting for the ground to open up and swallow me.

Time stood still for a while and then out of the blue a strange memory surfaced. I was scrambling into a small crawlspace with girl in a white dress and a blue garland round her neck. For a second, I was tempted to go back and tell them everything I knew. I held my tongue, because it felt like everything and nothing. At the gate I turned. There was a bitter taste in my mouth and I gritted my teeth.

'Thanks for coming,' I said.

Julie turned at the kitchen door; her cold eyes could have turned me to stone.

'From what mum's said, I think Suzanne was the one you really wanted to see.'

Her words felt like a punch to the stomach and I stood dejected as the girls waved a hurried goodbye and disappeared into the house. Carol moved closer to me, her soft features contrite, as if to say, well, we didn't see that coming.

'There was no need to…'

I finished the sentence for her.

'…be so belligerent? Maybe I've learnt an important lesson today. Don't go messing with your past.'

I walked briskly away, mulling over the conversations of the last hour, a meeting that had left more questions than answers. I felt drained, my integrity smashed into a thousand pieces.

Why didn't you come?

-

That evening I met Amber at The Windmill, a pub that did not entirely live up to its name, more Hansel and Gretel than Don Quixote. I found her perched like an exotic bird, her trademark blonde ponytail hanging down to the small of her back. She swiveled on her stool to face me, excitement etched on her freshly tanned face.

'You took your time.'

I tried to look cheerful.

'I walked.'

'How did it go?'

I eased myself onto the stool next to her and my shoulders slumped. I couldn't keep up the charade any longer.

'I'm not sure it was a roaring success.'

She hugged me.

'Amazing! Well, you proved us all wrong didn't you?'

She clearly thought I was clowning around and fluttered her eyelashes.

'Didn't they still fancy you? No hugs and kisses, no swapping of telephone numbers over a glass of Chardonnay?'

I hung my head in my hands. I was utterly disheartened and could do without being patronised. My voice had an edge.

'I could do with a proper drink.'

She placed her hand over mine.

'Well you can't. Can I have a Bloody Mary please, no vodka?'

I nodded to the barman as a nervous tick began in the corner of my left eye. She rummaged in her purse for some coins.

'Well?'

'It was an unmitigated disaster. I've never felt so awkward in my life. By the end I wanted to climb into a dark hole and hide. I was so embarrassed for Carol.'

Her eyes widened and she placed a consoling arm round my shoulder.

'Oh god, I'm sorry.'

My lips curled into a smirk.

'A little mutual respect wouldn't have a gone amiss, they made me feel this small.'

I pinched the air between thumb and forefinger. She nibbled thoughtfully on a bar snack.

'I can't believe it. Do you want to talk about it?'

I peppered my drink heavily with Tabasco and Worcestershire sauce and sucked long and hard through the straw.

'I didn't warm to either of them and from the moment we were introduced, I sensed a detachment and certain aloofness. We never got round to discussing the cruise, and if they did remember me, they were saying zip. Sara just stood in the background like a wet fish, chewing her hair.'

She swirled her wine round the glass.

'You went to tell your story and that's all you could do. By the way, what did they look like now? Were they pretty?'

I put my glass down.

'Absolutely not. They were country girls, a bit drab looking.'

'How did they react when you told them how you found them? They must have thought it was a bit spooky; it is an unbelievable story.'

I wiped my lip with a napkin.

'They just didn't get it. In fact, I'm sure they thought I was some kind of predatory stalker.'

She raised an eyebrow.

'A stalker! Well I don't think you'll be seeing them again.'

We both stared into space. The uncomfortable silence was only broken when Amber thumped her fist on the bar.

'That is so fucking rude!'

The barman stopped in mid glass clean and I purposely hovered my head over my drink. I didn't want to be blacklisted like Peter had been for coarse and vulgar language, although the fact it came from Amber's pretty mouth might have let us off the hook. I took a deep breath. In a matter of seconds I went from victim to full off-loading mode.

'Julie was confrontational from the start, as if she was spoiling for a fight. I showed them the proof, but I might as well have been speaking a foreign language. And after that it all went downhill very fast.'

She bristled with nervous energy.

'If I was in their shoes, I'd have been a little more gracious. It's not every day…'

I nodded in agreement.

'I think Julie thought I was having some form of midlife crisis and that I spent my time looking up old flames on Friends Reunited.'

She lowered her voice just in time.

'Fucking cheek, you were only being civil because you thought they'd be interested. Well, a midlife crisis? Debatable. I did find you looking at a Harley Davidson recently.'

My attempt to laugh ended up more of a snort of derision.

'I haven't ridden a motorbike since I was seventeen. I think they're bloody dangerous and there's no way on earth I'm getting a Harley when I have a young daughter.'

She swivelled on her stool and turned towards me.

'Well that's good to know. I still can't believe how they reacted.'

I squeezed her arm a little too enthusiastically and Amber pulled away.

'I was made to feel like some sex-starved monster and, check this out… she asked me if I had tried to contact all the girls who had signed the card!'

She choked on her drink and threw me an incredulous look.

'And what about the dreams? Did you tell them that you thought they were something to do with Suzanne?'

'No, I didn't mention it. If I had, they probably would have suggested I go and get some psychiatric help.'

She spent a minute in deep thought and her tone became a little more philosophical.

'Look, we all grow up and change don't we? We're never the same people we were before. Were they married?'

'I'm not sure, we didn't get round to discussing husbands and families.'

She shrugged her shoulders.

'You know, I feel partly responsible for getting you into all this.'

'It's not your fault.'

She grabbed my arm.

'Hang on. What about Suzanne?'

'She didn't come. It was probably for the best. You know what, I'm done with it all now.'

I threw some bar snacks into my mouth.

'Listen, it's ending here, no more delving into the past.'

She toyed with a beer mat.

'Maybe you're right.'

My voice cracked.

'Maybe it would have been different if I'd met Suzanne. I know you don't understand why, but I wanted to meet her, to find out who she had become. Was she married? Did she have a career? Was she happy? Do you understand…? I don't know what I'm saying.'

I stared into her eyes.

'Look, I want to apologise for being so fixated with her of late.'

She kissed me on the tip of my nose.

'I understand how this has affected you.'

I was on the verge of tears.

'If it hadn't been for you, I probably would have gone mad.'

Her eyes welled up.

'Listen, those Keen girls don't know what they're missing. If I'd been in their shoes, I would have been utterly intrigued by your story and dying to meet you.'

She caressed my cheek with a warm hand. I felt like a broken man.

'Will you come back and stay?'

She looked down, regretfully.

'I can't tonight, early start. Come on, I'll give you a lift.'

I was met at my front door by Lizzie, the farmer's youngest daughter.

'Everything OK?'

Lizzie picked up her school bag crammed with books.

'Hope was fine, we read "The Snow Pony" again.'

'I'm going to have to get her some more books, aren't I?'

Lizzie nodded in agreement.

'Thanks for staying late, hang on a second.'

I rummaged in my pockets and handed her an extra fiver.

'Night, night.'

I watched Lizzie walk across the paddock until she was safely through the courtyard gate.

-

I was unable to shrug off my melancholy mood, my emotions were in freefall and I couldn't stop thinking about Suzanne. I crept upstairs and lay on the bed and by the light of a luminous moon, a helter-skelter of images filled the void and I returned to the point where the story began 18 months ago: the discovery in the loft.

Through all of this an undercurrent had flowed, of something not quite right, something I couldn't quite put my finger on. Unable to sleep, I replayed the key conversations I'd had recently with my mother and Mrs Keen: was it possible they were both hiding something? I reached over and turned the radio on. The gravelly voice of a night-time disc jockey introduced a hit from the early 1970s. The volume was low, the faint music was familiar and I drowsed halfway between slumber and sleep, while the melodic chorus played over and over again in my head.

"We've got a thing going on
We both know that it's wrong
But it's much too strong
To let it go now…"

I hadn't heard this song since…since when?

Cocooned in my bed, my mind started to drift, like a listless lifeboat caught in a current. I felt myself travelling back in time, propelled by the warm trade winds. The soulful voice crooned on.

"Me and Mrs Jones…"

I was back on the ship. I was running barefoot along a labyrinth of thickly carpeted passageways. I could smell the sweet air laced with traces of spicy food and cigar smoke, and through the walls I could hear the distant hum of the ship's engines. I stood in a deserted lounge, the security lighting pulsed on and off, its reflection casting an eerie glow over the silent, cavernous room. I crouched on all fours and felt along the bulkhead. The lever was stiff, but the hatch opened and I half stumbled, half crawled into the crawlspace behind. Inside the fetid room, seaside odours of fish and chips and diesel clogged my nostrils. I called out, like an animal following a feral scent…

I opened my eyes. The last tendrils of the dream ebbed away and I was free from its grasp at last. Out of the bedroom window, the sun was rising and the room gradually filled with light. I pulled on scruffy track pants and, careful not to wake Hope, I tiptoed downstairs. I made myself a milky hot chocolate and sat at the breakfast bar allowing my sluggish mind to wake. I sipped the sweet drink and gazed across at a collage of old photographs in a glass frame; a previous life, in another place.

On a shelf below was the photograph of me taken on location in Morocco. Why did Anna hate that one so much? Was she jealous because we all looked so happy or was it because she saw my alter ego, my other self? The one she hated…

In a trance-like state I retrieved the menu card from the kitchen dresser. My hand trembled slightly and I had an overriding desire to light a match, to destroy the Oriana and all its memories for a second time. Instead I read out the children's names, like a roll call of the dead: Nicky Porter, Robin Bull, Jacqueline Marks, David and John Bull, James Cooper, Julie Shaxon, Twig, alias Robert Tyler, and Julie, Suzanne and Sara Keen. I wondered what happened to the rest of the gang. I cradled my mug, feeling the heat on my fingertips and read on.

'First squiggle on the moon.'

What a strange phrase that was and it annoyed the hell out of me that I would never know what it meant. My fingers traced across the page to the Keen's address and phone number, indelible proof that we were all on the ship together. I imagined our parents sitting round the dinner table, laughing and joking, drunk on free wine and spirits. Peter, Brenda, Chris and Hal, and the Keens. Did each family have their own card signed that night? And if so, what secrets would remain buried?

What do you want me to see?

Through the window the sun rose, a wondrous pink and orange glow caressing my eyes; it felt like the beginning of time. The golden rays seeped into every sinew and my whole body tingled. It was as if I'd been transported back in time, become what I was before, a mop-haired teenager, all raging hormones and awkwardness, the leader of the E deck gang. I had been popular, especially with the girls, and of course there had been one special one. I stifled a nervous laugh: is that what this was all about, innocent fumbles and flights of fancy in the dark?

In the shower, the song's melody stayed with me; couples always had their songs. Anna and I did: the song playing on the juke box when you first met, the first song you kissed to, the song outside a café on a perfect summer's day, the song you broke up to. Anna always wanted to dance to Spandau Ballet's 1980s classic, True. It's funny how it takes a soppy song to make you remember. I let the water power over me, its cleansing force driving the past away.

21

The red post van drove off in a cloud of dust and I walked down to the gate. I casually sifted through the Saturday post: bills, bank statements, junk mail and a white, hand-addressed envelope. Puzzled, I tore it open. Inside were three sheets of paper.

The pages were covered in a delicate swirling hand of blue ink that was smudged in places. I went into the garden sat on a bench, warmed by the morning sun and I began to read.

Dear Paul,

I am unsure if you are expecting this letter? It's been such a long time. You are probably wondering why I am writing to you now, and why I decided not to come with my sisters. Part of me did want to meet you but in my own time.

First things first. I must apologise for the frosty reception you received from my sister Julie. Don't ask me how I found out, I just did. We don't always see eye to eye these days and have not been close since dad left.(there's another story to tell you one day) Julie has been under immense pressure emotionally recently, but it's no excuse. We've had words.

Mum called me to say she had met you at Middlewood. I must say I didn't believe her at first. What trick of fate, what an unbelievable chain of events brought you to Cheshire and our past life.

I can't believe all these years later you found out where our family lived, where we all grew up. (Consequently I knew where to send this letter.) I find it slightly unnerving to think of you living next door to our old house (where I have a mixture of good and bad memories) walking the same lanes, visiting the same shops, meeting the same people. What are the chances of that happening after 30 odd years?

Mum didn't say if you were married or in a relationship, although she said you had children. You did better than me, barren as a desert. I'm not sad though. I'm not sure I was maternal enough. I hope the contents of this letter don't pose any tricky explanations to your partner if she should read it. I'm sure she would understand we were only innocent teenagers back then.

How are you enjoying life in the North West? I hope you are not turning into a Northern bore? There are too many of them up here already. I married one! Only joking. Anyway back to your incredible story, and your admirable investigative prowess. You're not a detective are you? Because it all sounds like something out of a 'Whodunit,' or in our case a how did you find me? Mum said you found a menu from the Oriana when you moved up here. Amazing. She said that we had all signed it, if we did I don't remember that! What did I write? Nothing too embarrassing I hope? Mum said you saw our old address and that was the catalyst that led you to find us all, and that you had photographs of us all together. I remember some of the gang. Do you? I wonder what happened to them all? Good things I hope.

Now for the real reason for this letter. I do want to meet you and I hope you still feel the same even after Julie's grilling. In fact considering what has happened it seems to be our destiny. I have fleeting memories of our time spent on the Oriana. It was a very special time, but I want you to know I am not looking to rekindle any past relationship. I am happily married and intend to stay so but some things happened on that holiday ... Do you remember what we did? Do you know what I am talking about? What we did? What I did? Can you forgive me? I haven't, but I hope even after all these years you can. If you're willing, I propose we meet a week from today at Carol's. I haven't supplied a phone number for obvious reasons. I think this should be our secret! I will concoct a story so as not to arouse suspicion and any gossip that may ensue. Look forward to seeing you and to quote James Taylor in 'Fire and Rain.' (Our song.)

'I always thought that I'd see you again.'
Love Suzanne
Ps I don't think you will recognise me now.

I read it through three times, slowly digesting the words.

Do you remember what we did...can you forgive me...

I felt my pulse quicken. I wished I could pick up the phone and ask her to help me fill the gaps in my fractured memory.

-

I crossed off the days and was like a faithful dog waiting for its owner to return. I wasn't myself, unable to concentrate on the simplest task, and when Amber phoned I was aloof and stand-offish. The following Saturday could not come quick enough, although it brought with it my greatest fear.

By the time the weekend arrived I was like a cat on a hot tin roof, my mind already second-guessing the answers I hoped to get. I was short-tempered, burnt the pancakes and made Hope go back and brush her teeth three times. A multitude of emotions threatened to paralyse me as my eyes scanned the stone out-buildings opposite.

Please don't have second thoughts and leave us both in limbo forever.

A few more minutes passed and my resolve wavered: part of me regretted opening this convoluted can of worms and for a split-second I considered walking away. I raised my hand to shield my face from the sun's golden rays. I was like a teenage boy on his first date, butterflies in the pit of my stomach, unsure whether I would be stood up. My tongue felt too big for my mouth and a bead of sweat ran along my upper lip; I'd been less nervous standing in line as I waited to be introduced to Prince Charles at Pinewood Studios.

A figure stepped out of the shadows. She wore a white dress and moved with a model's poise gracefully across the courtyard towards me. She was smaller than I imagined and for once there was nothing remotely Anna-like in her appearance. She was dressed smartly, so different from her sisters. I reflected momentarily how my dead wife would interpret this curious reunion. Would it be a closure of sorts?

I studied Suzanne in more detail as she approached, but her angular face was not familiar to me. I smiled, an expression of wonderment tinged with trepidation. She raised her sunglasses, pushing them back into her neat platinum hair. She was close, and I felt her physical presence.

Flesh and blood.

She smiled back, a mischievous smile from thirty years ago. I blinked. Sunspots formed in front of my eyes. Was I daydreaming?

No. This was no longer a fantasy; she was real.

We stood opposite each other, heads inclined, like two swans mirroring each other's movements and her eyes searched mine for recognition. She smelled of honey and orange and I wondered who would be the first to break the spell: who would be the first to speak?

We both started talking at the same time.

'Did you get my...?

'I got your...'

Suzanne hesitated for a moment before she placed a small object into my palm. Her words caught in the wind.

'I'm sorry.'

I looked down into her eyes, still inviting after all these years.

'For what?'

She swallowed and her voice was thick with emotion.

'It's been on a long journey.'

APRIL 1974

Suzanne's Story

Each day blurred into another until the ship reached the tranquil waters of the Caribbean. The weather gradually became more oppressive and the screens around the main pool created a cauldron of sweltering heat. She chose to wear her favourite pink bikini which accentuated her blossoming figure and budding breasts; convincing her mother to buy it from the ship's boutique had been another thing entirely, because she'd already pushed her luck with frequent requests for a necklace.

Today she wore her latest acquisition, a delicate gold chain, with a pendant in the shape of a clenched fist. The sales assistant explained how the fist, with thumb protruding, was an ancient sign of tribal fertility, which amused Suzanne no end.

The previous night they had watched American Graffiti and today they were the girls from the strip, gossiping, flirting and, much to their parents' annoyance, chewing gum. She lowered her sunglasses and watched the boys dive into the pool. It was crowded and occasionally she got splashed, but she wasn't bothered; it was all part of the fun. She was not consciously thinking about sex, but nevertheless she was aware of the differences in the boys' bodies, their toned limbs and flat muscular stomachs and the bulge in their trunks. One older boy in black trunks emerged dripping from the water and she couldn't help but stare a little too long. Some larger than others she thought.

Out of the corner of her eye, Suzanne spotted his
mother in her familiar leopard-skin bikini. The
woman was the colour of caramel and Suzanne
studied every minute movement of her limbs as she
walked seductively round the pool. Suzanne was
relieved his father was nowhere to be seen; only
yesterday he had caught them canoodling in the
cabin. They weren't doing anything improper, but all
the same he blew a gasket; children should be up on
deck in the fresh air, not fooling around in the
gloomy confines of their cabin, apparently.

She enjoyed kissing him, it made her insides feel
strangely liquid and warm. She liked him a lot, but
was wary not to use the L word. No, that could wait
until he'd done what she asked. They had found their
hideaway when the weather was inclement, when it
was too cold for outdoor games. Someone had seen a
film about stowaways and Twig suggested they
search the lower decks looking for illicit travellers.
They all knew it was forbidden to go below G deck,
below the staff quarters and into the hold, so the two
of them headed for the deserted forward lounges
where during the day the grown-ups played cards.
They discovered the storage compartment by luck
and the boy's excitement was obvious, even though it
was full of lifejackets and maintenance equipment
and reeked of diesel.

'Come and look, this would make a great hiding
place!'

He disappeared back into the dark, claustrophobic
space, imitating the tobacco-chewing sheriff in "Live
and Let Die". He was very good at mimicking people
with odd mannerisms and she liked that quirkiness

about him. He was funny, with an inner confidence, unlike Twig who just liked showing off.

She watched his mother wrap her daughter in a blue towel with a grey dolphin on it and Suzanne's eyes were drawn to the beautiful charm bracelet that hung from her wrist.

Then it happened. A glint of sunlight reflected off the woman's left hand.

Suzanne heard herself gasp and found she was unable to shake her gaze. She knew in that split second she had to have it. It was the most beautiful ring she had ever seen; of course, he was completely disinterested in what adornments his mother wore. He was more interested in what film they were going to see next or sneaking up to their hideaway for a late-night snog. She knew she would have to work on him and bide her time.

Later, in the dark storage room, their hands and mouths explored each other.

'Do you think we will see each other again after the cruise?' she'd enquired over the incessant drone of the engines.

His lips were pressed against hers and she had to turn her mouth to the side to catch her breath.

'Of course.'

'London is so far away, perhaps I could get the train.'

'Would your parents let you?'

Suzanne held him tight, enjoying the intimacy that she craved.

'I wish we could stay on this ship forever.'

'Me too, I don't want go back to school.'

Suzanne's hormones surged uncontrollably, emotions connecting then disconnecting at a rapid rate. At that moment it made perfect sense. A new adventure. That's what lovers would do.

He seemed to read her mind.

'We could go wherever the ship was going next.'

Her mature brain had control now and she fell into a dreamy state of eternal love.

'Let's make a pledge.'

He hadn't grasped what she meant.

'Like a pact you mean. I saw this film where a girl and boy cut their hands with a penknife and pressed their palms together so their blood mixed.'

Boys could be so stupid. She fought back her dark side. She told him she was thinking of something a little more romantic.

'Like what?' he'd replied, like a typical young boy.

Then it was time to show her hand.

'Your mother wears the most exquisite ring I've ever seen.'

He sneaked his hand under her top.

'It was her granny's.'

She pushed his hand away.

'If I got married, I'd want one like that.'

Then the other voice, the thieving magpie in her head spoke, and she asked him to do the unthinkable.

'Get it for me.'

He froze.

'You're not serious? Why do you want a stupid ring anyway?'

She realised he would need some gentle persuasion.

'We could pretend it was an engagement ring.'

'Engagement! Isn't that like being married?'

'You said you loved me…'

He hesitated for a few seconds, weighing up her demand.

'Anyhow, she hardly ever takes it off.'

She persisted with her wily game.

'You'll have to watch her and come up with a plan.'

He could be stubborn as a mule sometimes and he stood his ground.

'It's stealing. And what happens if I get caught?'

She remained calm and used every ounce of her girlish charm.

'Don't worry. We'll only borrow it for an hour and then you can put it back.'

She had meant to give it back, but things had changed so quickly.

They met the next morning outside the Kids' Club. It was Twig's birthday and there was bunting hanging across the doorway. Inside, the room was full of noise and activity as everyone prepared for the party that afternoon. She grabbed a rail as the ship pitched in the swell.

'Well, do you think you can get it?'

'It's going to be difficult,' he replied.

It was the penultimate night of the cruise and although her tone was sympathetic, she was controlling things now. She knew how fickle boys were and how easy it was to manipulate them with the offer of feeling her up. She quite liked his amateur attempts at fondling.

'I'll let you go to second base again.'

His eyes lit up.

'OK, I'll try, but I'm not promising anything. Mum and dad have asked me to babysit my sister after dinner. If they find out I've left her on her own in the cabin, I'm dead.'

'Don't worry, we'll have it back before she knows it's missing.'

She kissed him properly with her tongue and hurried off to lunch in the Monkey Bar with her family.

-

She waited in the dark for what seemed an eternity, praying that his parents had not decided to go to bed early, condemning him to solitary confinement, or had caught him red-handed. If that was the case it was over, there was no time left.

She had almost resigned herself to the purgatory of lost love when in the gloomy silence she heard a hinge creak. In the darkness she lay very still, her heart racing. When she heard his voice, her whole body tingled with anticipation, although at the same time she had a burning need to tell him she had discovered something dreadful, something that changed everything. He reached into his pocket and opened his hand.

'Shine the light so I can see it.'

Earlier, she had been sent back to her own cabin to find her parents' camera. While she searched, she came across a pink envelope tucked neatly out of sight in a holdall. It was scented and she toyed with it until curiosity got the better of her and she withdrew the single sheet of note paper.

Her face flushed, for she knew immediately who had written it. She had heard her mother mention the Captain's fancy dress party and the Cat Woman, who had flirted so outrageously with the Captain, the woman from London who turned heads in her skimpy leopard-print bikini, who stole the march on glamorous evening wear, with a host of fashionable outfits. She had heard the hushed whispers and seen the stolen glances, but she just presumed her father had become intoxicated by the ship's carefree and relaxed atmosphere. She didn't understand that this alluring woman might be a threat. She had remembered her mother's terse comment.

'Fancy woman from fancy London.'

She put the note and its treacherous declarations of lust back in the envelope and slotted it back in its hiding place.

-

After they left the crawlspace, she blindfolded him and took him to the pool, where only the day before she had seen the crew secure the cover loosely. She knew exactly what she was going to do. It was only meant to be a game, but the angry voice in her head told her to do it and under a canopy of brilliant white stars she led him to the edge and pushed him into the dark void.

-

When the ship docked in a cool, misty Southampton, everything moved so quickly. The relaxed atmosphere of the preceding weeks vanished in a blur of hurried bag packing, subdued goodbyes and onward travel arrangements. Many had travelled the length of the country and in an instant they were all disembarking, going their separate ways by car, taxi or train. She scanned the faces of dozens of children as they scurried past with their parents, but there was no sign of the boy or his family. They had gone. She moved in the direction of the station with her parents, the ring safely hidden in a heart-shaped jewellery box at the bottom of her suitcase. Her chance for forgiveness had slipped away.

APRIL 1974

Paul's Story

After dinner his parents returned to their cabin. His father reeked of whisky and tobacco and he stood impatiently by the door waiting for his mother to change.

He lay on his bunk and watched his mother remove the ring before applying cream to her hands. Then his parents started to argue. Something had gone missing and he cowered as his father flew into a rage and said something about finding the fucking porter. Distracted and agitated, his mother popped a few items into a clutch bag and left with his drunken father in tow. Watching from his bunk he couldn't believe his luck; in her haste his mother had forgotten to put the ring back on.

He waited a few minutes and when he thought it was safe, he checked on his sister. He heard her shallow rhythmic breathing and happy that she was asleep, he slipped silently off the bunk to the floor. He knew what he was about to do was wrong and he hesitated for a moment, considering the consequences.

'Under no circumstances leave the cabin and remember to lock the door securely when we've gone.'

He approached the sink. If he was caught, he decided he would blame the girl. With the ring in his pocket, he took one last glance at his sleeping sister and slipped barefoot out into the corridor. He hurried past cabin after cabin, catching snippets of after-dinner laughter from open doors. He continued upwards, stairwell after stairwell, deck after deck, heading for the Veranda deck. He reached a safety door and exited out onto an external walkway where the wind whipped his thin brown legs as he ran towards the cosseted warmth of the forward Ocean Lounge. Eventually he reached his destination and crouched down and felt for the handle. He pulled it and the hatch opened.

In a blissful charade he threaded the ring onto Suzanne's finger and they made their solemn vows. If necessary, they would cross the length and breadth of the country to see each other again and when the winter nights drew in, and they lay in their beds hundreds of miles from each other, they would remember this night and it would bring them close again.

-

A sheep bleated, bringing me back to the present. Suzanne dabbed at her eyes with a tissue.

'I made you do it...I promised to give it back...'

I looked at the object in my hand and shook my head in disbelief.

'I don't remember. I don't remember anything.'

Suzanne's hand lingered on my arm. It was like a jolt of electricity.

My next words were no more than a whisper.

'I stole it?'

Suzanne's eyes were full of remorse.

'Yes.'

I was dazed; my head didn't feel like it was attached to my body anymore.

'I...'

'I made you take it and then I deceived you, and for that I am truly sorry. I let others take the blame and when the cruise ended, I meant to find you. Honestly I did.'

The lift plummeted. For a second I thought I was going to be sick, as the staggering enormity of what had happened sunk in.

'Oh God! Why didn't we own up?'

Suzanne reached out, her eyes were of azure pools of redemption.

'That's why I'm here now I guess.'

Curiosity killed the cat. Satisfaction brought it back.

She held my gaze.

'I've dreamt of this reunion for so long. My grandmother was right, you never forget your first love.'

I guided her through the gate and back to the normality of a trampoline and children's toys.

'Come on, I'll introduce you to Hope and Lottie.'

'We have so much to...I need to tell you everything.'

I placed an arm round her shoulder.

'My mother will be...'

'Wait! First I need to tell you about my father.'

Suzanne started to cry. Not waves of exaggerated sobbing, just a gentle trickle of teardrops.

'I'd always been my father's favourite. Not that he ever told me to my face, I just knew I was. My father had grand ideas for his middle daughter, so maybe in those early years he pushed me a little too hard. We were very similar, both able to love unconditionally, yet we both possessed a dark side; for me, it was a lone voice that could tilt my world with frightening consequences. I knew about my father's womanising, hated those dirty women, planning all types of sordid ends for them. And then he left. Why didn't he pick up the phone or write to me? Surely he hadn't stopped loving me? I remembered my mother's life had been torn apart, our family's agony prolonged forever. Yet somehow we survived. My mother never remarried, maybe she thought it was impossible to love someone else when she never knew if, like a soldier missing in action, her husband, our father may one day return. It was the not knowing, not being able to grieve, not being able to move on. I prayed night after night, that if he was alive, one day he would return.'

Suzanne fought back tears.

'Because I never stopped loving him.'

I took a deep breath.

'And what about the ring?'

'In my dreamy adolescence I presumed at some point your parents would call and you would forgive me. Of course, the reality was that we never did meet up again. In my naivety, I thought about sending the ring back in the post, then the bit of paper with your address on it was mislaid and any further contact was lost forever, I thought. The years accelerated by and I often worried that I would return home from school one day to be met by stern-faced parents waving a letter in my face. I never confided in anyone about the ring, never told my sisters and only as time passed did I sometimes feel confident about wearing it. After I got married, my husband presumed it had been in my family all along. No-one ever asked awkward questions. For many years I had no idea of its true value and it was only after a meeting with my insurance broker that I discovered how rare the pearl and its setting were. I remember that day very clearly, how I felt awash with a mixture of emotions: wonderment, sadness, but most of all guilt. It is a truly priceless piece and absolutely irreplaceable. I occasionally ruminated about the right course of action, toying with various schemes. Once I nursed the idea of turning myself in to the local police as a petty criminal, in the hope that the ring would find its way onto Crimewatch and you, or someone, somewhere might recognise it and call the show. I never plucked up the courage to do it.'

'To love and to cherish. Til death do us part. Those were my parting words to you.'

Suzanne laughed half-heartedly.

'We were just acting out adolescent fantasies. Although ironically, the words have a ring of truth about them now. On numerous occasions I've lain awake at night, imagining this moment and what it would feel like, and finally, after all these years, the unthinkable has happened.'

Suzanne paused and blew her nose with a pink tissue.

'My undoing, a solitary menu card! What an unbelievable fluke, who keeps such things?'

I encouraged Suzanne to continue, for it was clear she was unburdening herself of decades of turmoil and angst.

'What were your feelings when your mother told you that I had contacted the family?'

Suzanne looked pensive.

'I had no idea how you'd react. How much did you know? How much did you remember? For all I knew, you could have been stalking me for years, eventually getting lucky with your move north. Inside I felt elated, of course I did. You were alive and well, and astonishingly, living within a stone's throw of our old family home in Cheshire. My mother thought it was coincidence, but I wasn't so sure. Many years ago I convinced myself that some things should always remain buried.'

The tears flowed again now and Suzanne sniffed them up.

'If I could go back, there are so many things I would change.'

Sometime in the future

Hope and I still live in the barn. The farmers keep
their distance, respectful of our privacy, but they have
a soft spot for my daughter and watch out for both of
us. Hope is still obsessed with horses and rides
regularly at a friend's house, where she has the loan
of a pony and the mucking out duties to go with it.
Last year, in a moment of madness, I agreed to
another dog; Hope chose a Cocker Spaniel, 16 weeks
of real trouble. Once a year we make the pilgrimage
down south to lay flowers on Anna's grave and Hope
keeps her mother updated with our progress by
writing our annual letter.

Sadly, my relationship with Amber cooled, but we
stayed friends. She was offered a job in Shanghai:
new challenges, new life. How could she resist? So
she closed her business, rented her cottage out and
left Monty behind in the UK with her mother. I saw
her off at the airport; there were no tears. We'd
shared some special moments, although we both
knew it was time for us to move on. She lives in a
smart duplex with a pool and Robyn attends an
international school in the suburbs. We keep in touch
via email and she says I can visit whenever I want.
One day I may take her up on the offer. Who knows
what the future will bring...maybe another cruise!

In spite of all that had gone before, I kept in touch
with Suzanne. Nothing serious, just very old friends
catching up. She plucked up the courage to tell me
about the incident in the pool, how a passing steward
had dragged me from the water just in the nick of
time; it's no wonder I was a reluctant swimmer. It

appeared my mother had no idea how close I came to death that night and even after a session with a hypnotist, I still had no memory of the bizarre sequence of events that night on the Oriana.

My mother had the ring altered and once again wore it on her engagement finger, fittingly I thought. Sadly, within a year the cancer returned and she fought it bravely to the end. I miss her every day. While sifting through her personal effects I came across a folder bound by a red ribbon. Inside were documents: receipts, photographs and a copy of her last will and testament. Amongst the reams of documents were a bundle of letters. I kept this one as it was unopened; it clearly had never been sent.

Dearest G

The holiday is nearly at an end now, what a thrilling episode it has been in our lives, what a ride! And made all the more special by meeting you. You have been so charming and sweet to me.

However I am still haunted by that terrible business a few nights ago. I feel numb, violated although I realise this is probably just an over-reaction! There can be only be one rational explanation, unless of course there are ghosts walking the decks at night, and I don't believe in ghosts.

On another note I apologise for my husband's behaviour. He is such a loutish bore, but it's the drink speaking. He is a man of low self-esteem, always felt he wasn't good enough and therefore sought solace in the demon spirit. To be perfectly honest, I don't know what I saw in him all those years ago. Just a physical thing, I think.

I will miss our special moments together – all too brief, all too delicious! I only wish it didn't have to end, but I fear it will and we will never see each other again. This will remain our secret, for neither of us can afford to sacrifice what we already have, can we?

Bon Voyage

J

PS Visit me in your dreams.

I took the letter and the menu card and placed them in a drawer with other treasured family mementos. I decided it was finally time to leave the ghosts in peace.

THE END

Read on for an exclusive extract from my next pedal-to-the-metal thriller out in late 2020…

The Bleed

'Maybe stories choose how they are told and who tells them.'

Karnard Kojouri

Prologue

'One last job' I'd said, because the last thing I wanted was to get sucked back in again…

…and then I was standing in a queue with the early evening commuters. I pulled a cold can from my backpack and through the drizzle watched traffic lights meld through the bus shelter glass.

I was looking forward to a chilled weekend and still buzzing from the stash Christian and I had found earlier. I remembered the monster Rolls, beating out Drake before it sped off from the vicinity of McDonald's car park and headed for the cements works and the river. Our luck, the small foil package lying amongst the burger wrappers in the gutter.

That car spelled trouble.

I flipped the ring pull at exactly the same moment the bus stop up ahead seemed to shudder and zoom in and out of focus. I clutched my chest and there was a searing pain that travelled from my shoulder, down through my groin and into my left leg. My world began to tilt and as I struggled for breath, I grasped the arm of an elderly lady next to me.

Lisa. I'm sorry…

The lady with the shopping stroller turned, a look of alarm on her wrinkled face. I dropped the half-full can of Stella and in what seemed like slow motion, the can spun and fizzed before it rolled under the wheels of an oncoming bus. A second later there was a roar, a rush of blood in my temples as the pavement rushed up to meet me.

My head whiplashed. Someone flicked a switch.

Darkness.

Paul Barrell is a keen sportsman and has skied all over the world.

He is a serial entrepreneur and has owned restaurants and wine companies. He is passionate about food and wine.

He came to writing later in life and writes about real events and people that have shaped his life.

His first book, Postcards from Pimlico, is currently being turned into a screenplay for TV.

He now lives in the Surrey hills with his wife and rescue dog Lottie.

Keep in touch with Paul:

www.paulbarrellauthor.wordpress.com

Twitter: @Paulbarrellauthor

Instagram: @Paulbarrellbooks

FB: Paulbarrellauthor

Also by Paul Barrell:

Postcards from Pimlico

Magnetic North